an anthology of evil men

esme oliver

Author of Smoke Drink F*#k

D1280207

An Anthology of Evil Men Copyright © 2018 by Esme Oliver

All Rights Reserved. No part of this book may be reproduced or transmitted in any form or by any means, electronic or mechanical, including photocopying, without permission in writing from the publisher.

This is a work of fiction. Names, characters, places and incidents are the product of the author's imagination or are used fictitiously. Any resemblance to actual events, locales or persons, living or dead, is coincidental.

For more information contact:
Riverdale Avenue Books
5676 Riverdale Avenue
Riverdale, NY 10471
www.riverdaleavebooks.com

Design by www.formatting4U.com
Cover by May Phan
Digital ISBN 9781626014800
Print ISBN 9781626014794

First edition, September 2018

Table of Contents

Author's Note

For decades, women have endured the 'evil' side of men whether it be in the kitchen, in the bedroom, in the workplace or somewhere in between.

I have been working on the Anthology of Evil men for over a decade drawing upon my wide-ranging experiences and finally was able to find my voice and tell these tales through a series of stories that can undoubtedly been shared with women of all ages, races and backgrounds. We have finally entered an age where women now have a voice. And, hopefully this book will encourage all women to stand up, be heard and attain the proper treatment they deserve in life.

Alex

I am two days out of college, I am 21 years old, and in Washington D.C. I have never lived outside Indiana where I grew up in a bucolic neighborhood with a creek bordering a one-acre backyard. Our house was near a field covered with blackberries that we would grab while rapidly riding bikes so we could later sell them to passersby.

My mom and her best friend had driven me here for an internship I had just landed in the U.S. House of Representatives. My apartment is bare, with one pale powder blue sofa, a small antiquated TV, a double bed in my bedroom, and a scale in the bathroom. Only five days ago, I had been living in a house full of girls—hundreds of them—and although I often felt alone there, especially late at night, when I would organize my closet and weigh myself on the scale, I never really had to be alone. There was *always* someone to go drinking with on a Thursday or even on a Sunday night—someone who wanted to make a run to Taco Bell.

As I unpack my J. Crew sweaters, T-shirts, and mostly oversized clothes, I realize that there is no one else here. My mom is gone. Most of my friends have migrated to Chicago. And I am totally alone now to figure it out…. what am I going to do with the rest of life?

1

The next day I get on the subway to go to work. I get lost on a subway platform. I get on the blue line instead of the orange line from the red line where I began. I should have practiced yesterday. I'm running late and already panicking. I'm to get off at the Capitol South stop—right near the House of Representatives where I am starting the first day of my Capitol Hill job as an intern to a Congressman from Indiana.

It's incredibly hot and crowded in the subway car. I can feel the beads of sweat dripping down into my bra and onto my stomach—and my size four skirt is tight around my waist. As the sweat trickles down it, I can feel the fat over my waistband, and I make a note to eat less today and weigh in when I get home.

I wonder if coming to DC was a good idea. Why am I doing this? What do I have to prove? I should have gone to Chicago with Andrew. I should have just gone with him—married him. That is what I should have done.

But as I get out of the scorching hot subway station, I look up and see the dome of the Capitol and it takes my breath away. At this point, I had only seen it on TV, but I realize that this is the place where the laws are made, and I want to write laws and change the world.

As an intern, a job you are blessed to have, you mainly sort mail and answer phones. There is some writing of letters to constituents too, but, by and large, it's pretty administrative and pretty boring.

But I got lucky. Things are moving fast around here, and a couple of people have quit recently so they need someone to help cover health care. I don't know *anything* about health care, but the people here seem to believe in me.

"Listen Esme, you are a bright girl. This is why we hired you." Abbe, my legislative director and new boss, who I immediately decide I will be one day, tells me this in a direct, matter-of-fact way.

"I've got an education bill to get to the floor. I'll help you if you get stuck, but you are on your own—we trust your judgment. And you better come up with some ideas. He's going to need to offer some amendments." She walks away.

That is it. There is no orientation here.

That night I go home to my apartment in Arlington, Virginia (I can't afford to live in the city) with lots of reports and pink and yellow highlighters jammed in my backpack. I don't even know where to start. I'm just so tired. And I just can't sit still for nine hours a day. I'm used to moving, shuffling my bookbag and AP Style book between classrooms on buildings sitting on top of hills. I miss college—my friends, our Thursday night at Jerry's, my boyfriend in Chicago who really isn't my boyfriend anymore because I refused to come with him even though I said I would do so at least three times. I even miss my classes. I'm so overwhelmed and so lonely. I am starting to really believe this whole thing was just a huge mistake.

Thank God I have one person in my life who is now here. Melanie arrived today. Melanie is my college sorority sister and life-long friend. We have both, for unrelated reasons, decided to move to Washington. Almost everyone else went to Chicago. We should have gone to Chicago, but we came here.

I take the subway home, rip off my high heels and lay on the sofa with a cold bottle of beer to my face and then to my lips. I down it and then another. I pop two pills—the pills I have taken since I can remember, the ones that are supposed to get me out of bed in the morning.

I am determined to take on these papers tonight and learn this stuff, but I am as lacking of effort as a lazy leaf on a still fall day. I want to call my mom and complain, but I can't even manage to dial the phone.

Melanie, who hasn't found a job yet, comes into the living room and sits next to me on the powder blue tattered sofa, the one piece of furniture we possess, other than our beds. Our parents "got us started," and then my father promptly cut me off. I have no idea how I'm going to pay for everything I need now.

"Hey. How was your first day?" She is all smiles and giggles.

"Horrible. I'm so tired. I have no idea what I'm doing." I push my bangs off my forehead.

"You're smart, Esme. You'll figure it out."

"No, no. You have no idea. They want me to do "health care"—which is so huge now, and I have no idea what any of this even means. And you should see these people I work with... they are so so unbelievably smart."

"You always do this. I don't why you do this."

I throw the papers in the air.

"I have so much reading to do. I'm going to be reading all week and this weekend."

"Well, you can't read all weekend."

"Why?" I put the beer back on my forehead. It's cool and wet, and I'm so hot—we don't have air conditioning yet. My dad told me to go into business—to work for a company. So, I ditched my journals and AP stylebook and learned how to use a calculator. I studied Economics diligently—learned about price elasticity of demand, the consumer price index and inflation. I persevered and got an A minus. But I always found myself looking out the window at the long blades of grass growing on the college lawn thinking about a story that I needed to write down. Economics wasn't working out for me. Dreamers find calculators cold company. This isn't where I was supposed to end up, but somehow this is where I landed.

"Because. We're going to go out!" She pulls up the window shades still beaming with late day sunlight.

I cover my face. I want the room to be dark.

"Where? I don't even know where to go."

"On Saturday. Rally in the Alley."

"What is 'rally in the alley'?"

"It's a big party downtown... in Georgetown on 23rd and M."

"What kind of party?"

"Just an all-day thing. Beers. Guys. People, you know. We need to get out. I'm gonna call Janey and Matt to see if they'll meet us." She slaps my leg. "Come on! Buck up."

I don't want think about to going out right now. I decide, as I often do when overwhelmed, that I'm going to quit. I always quit. I'm a huge fan of quitting. If something isn't working, why stay in it?

I'm not cut out for this. I should have just gone with Andrew and got a job in advertising. A normal life. I want to call him now more than ever, but instead, after smoking two cigarettes, I crawl into bed. I skip dinner. I weigh myself. I'm up two pounds. Already. Fuck. I am not going to have anytime time to workout now let alone go to step aerobics twice a day. I have to sit at that bloody desk for nine hours a day while the fat just piles up on my hips and thighs.

The next day I succeed at the subway. I make it to work this time without any problems.

As I walk in through the back door, I'm nervous but try to be upbeat and pleasant.

"Good morning." I state loudly with a smile.

I greet the office. But, everyone is already buried in their work—all the letters, and newspapers and scheduling requests, magazines. There is just so much to read.

"Hey." A couple of people look up from their desks to acknowledge me, but no one is talking, and no one is going to talk to me much more today.

I sit at my desk in the open area where four legislative aides reside. There are already four messages written on little yellow paper on my desk.

"Who are these for? Me?" I ask Abbe, who is wearing a perfectly tailored pale pink suit and a thick pearl necklace. She looks like Jackie Kennedy only with chunky black glasses and with a more acerbic demeanor. I can tell she is super smart, and I decide that I will study her, learn everything from her, win her over.

She pauses, looks up from her keyboard, sliding the glasses down her nose.

"They are people who want to talk to Edward about health care, but instead they are going to talk to you."

"Me?"

"Yes. No one gets to talk to him—unless they are a CEO or a president of a university." She goes back to typing her floor statement. I don't know what to say to these people. But I don't want to bother her anymore.

That day, I meet the Congressman... right after witnessing him throw a pen at a woman staffer's head and then telling her to shut up. I wonder if he is going to throw something at me.

"Congressman?" I am standing outside his office peeking my head in.

Abbe pulls my arm and leads me into his big circular office that is draped with American flags and photos of black Labrador Retrievers, "This is Esme, our new intern. You remember her resume... Meeting her..."

He doesn't.

"Yes. Yes. Of course." He stands up. He is handsome, salt and pepper, lanky—a bit younger than my father. He seems confident but angry. And that makes me nervous.

"Good to meet you!" He extends his hand. Short stubby fingers. Shakes my hand firmly. My long fingers do not fit well with his short fingers. I think this is a sign—we are not a good match.

"Hello Congressman. Very nice to meet you."

"No, call me Ed." Wide teeth smile. He looks like a politician.

"Okay.... Ed."

It feels weird to call a Member of Congress by his first name. My parents always said it was rude to call adults by their first name. But I do what he says.

After the obligatory meeting with Ed, I go back to my desk and read, highlight. and prepare a briefing book for the next days' hearing on health care reform. I stare out my window and look onto the Capitol where I can see bodies running around. I think about how much I want this day to end so I can have a drink and a smoke. I think about the upcoming weekend, which is actually going to be fun because Melanie is here.

* * *

"Esme, hey, are you ready?"

It's Saturday, about noon. Melanie comes into my sparse room and sits on my bed, which is draped with a peach and beige reversible comforter. A Claude Monet print hangs on the wall above it. The Rally in the Alley, the all-day drink-a-thon has begun, and she has convinced me to go with her.

I slip on my oversized lavender sweater and black leggings. It is summer but an unusually cool day, and I'm not one to wear something undersized or even something with a regular fit. As I frequently do, I am trying to conceal the vast majority of my body.

"Come on, let's go," Melanie shuts off my bedroom light.

"God. Why do you keep listening to that 10,000 Maniacs song over and over again? Come on. Let's go!"

I grab my purse. My keys. My cigarettes. My lip gloss. My "staples."

We are off.

We meet our friends from college, Janey and Matt, at a divey smokey bar and immediately start pounding bottles of cheap Miller Light. We are making about $20,000 a year, except Melanie, but she is subsidized by her parents. I am living off rapidly dwindling funds from my father—I haven't even gotten my first paycheck yet. We can't afford to both drink and eat. I am eating black bean soup or rice most nights for dinner. Today, we choose to drink instead.

We start pounding beers. Matt orders shots of Tequila. We pound those too. I look at my watch and I see it's only 4:00, and we're pretty wasted. I'm starting to think maybe I am going to like D.C.

We move outside to the patio because there is more room, our dewy brown bottled beers in hand. . The air is cold and misty and it starts to lightly drizzle. I pull my hair back into a ponytail. I pull out the rubber band I always carry for emergencies like this— my hair is going to go curly and frizzy. I continue drinking my beer.

"Shit, it's starting to rain. " I turn to Melanie.

"No, no, it's not going to rain." She tilts her almost empty beer bottle toward her mouth. "Come on, let's get another."

"I think we need some more shots!" Matt holds his left arm high, motioning the waitress, "Five tequilas!"

Suddenly, someone shoves me. My left side. I turn to look, and there he is.

The man who will occupy and consume every minute of my life for the next year.

"Hey. Sorry about that." He looks at me and pushes his friend who is directly behind him.

"My friend is a real asshole." He raises up his beer.

Black and red plaid button down. Khakis. Blonde hair tousled as if he had just been in the salty ocean. Aquamarine eyes. He's broad and built like a football player. I feel so small standing right next to him.

I think he is the most gorgeous guy I have ever seen. In fact, I have seen him so many times before.

The guys push again, and I fall back into Mel. She has no tolerance for bawdy boys. As I turn to look at his friends with equal disdain, he grabs my elbow and smiles so wide—the crinkles from the corners of his mouth hitting his eyes.

"Hey," He looks at me, straight into my eyes.

"Hey. Did anyone ever tell you... that... you have the most beautiful green eyes?"

He is drunk. I can tell as his chest is pressing into me. I can smell the beer on his breath and cigarettes on the collar of his shirt.

"Yes. And they are *blue*." I smile.

"Blue, really? Well, I'm drunk." He laughs. But, you've got some great eyes."

His friend, Nick, who I also recognize, pushes against him again which makes him fall into me.

"Quit it, man! What the fuck?" He yells back at Nick. The bar is crowded now, and everyone is pushing everyone.

I focus intensely on his face. Yes. It really is him.

"So, what's your name—girl with the great *blue* eyes?"

"Don't you know who I am?" I squint. Our college was small and cliquey—surely he must have seen me there, at some point.

"No... I just think you have great eyes." He laughs, and his chest collapses into mine again.

I notice a small clump of blond hair popping out from his under shirt, just above the hollow in his neck. My mind is like a camera—I take pictures of everything on him. The shoes. The plaid shirt. The clumps of hair in the hollow of his neck. The Fossil watch hanging loosely on his wrist.

The bar is getting crowded, and I have to arch my back to keep my balance. Everyone is pushing into us.

"We went to college together," I feel the warm blood rush to my face—realizing that he has no idea who I am.

"Really, what is your name? He looks surprised.

"I know your name!" I exclaim.

"Well, what is it then?" He rubs the coarse stubble on his chin.

"Alex. Alex Carrington."

"Fuck. You do know me. What is your name?"

"Esme…. Esme Oliver!" I shout my name over the all the noise in the bar.

"Hmmm. That sounds familiar. I feel like I have read about you." He smiles.

"Were you on Student Senate?" He cocks his head to the left side with inquisitive eyes.

"Yes. I was vice-president."

"Ah, yes, your name sounds familiar. I think I remember reading something about you in *The Post.*"

Finally, he remembers something about me.

"I know who *you* are." I blurt suddenly. "You dated P. J. Jacobs."

All those stupid southern girls thought it was necessary to have two names—Sara Elizabeth, Mary Kate, and even cooler to use their initials. Patricia Jane was one of them and was in the oldest and most prestigious sorority house where all the girls of privilege came together.

I used to see them walking around campus holding hands. Her chic black bob and lithe olive legs moving effortlessly in a long white sundress with flip-flops. They looked so elegant together. You couldn't really stop staring or stop envying everything about them.

"P.J.? Wow. How did you know that?" He looks at me intently.

"I remember.... I mean I kind of knew her. I used to see you guys sometimes at Clyde's."

"Really? Did you hang out at Clyde's?"

"Sometimes. "

"Well, she's a fucking psycho." He looks around left to right, "so if you see her come in here, we're bolting. She's gotten so out of control since we graduated."

"Does she live here?"

"Yeah, in McLean. She's from here."

P.J. Jacobs, like Alex Carrington, grew up *here*, attending the top prep schools, taking subway trains to the mall at age eight and hanging with kids who had their birthday parties at the Ritz Carlton. She had the perfect black hair—flat as a tabletop, straight as the letter I. I used to stare at her. Covet her. I could see why she got him. She was perfect in every way.

I change the subject. I don't want to know why she was psycho. She probably wasn't. He probably just wouldn't marry her, which is what all those girls wanted, expected, after graduation.

"You were in *The Post* too. I remember reading that piece about you... getting arrested for stealing a Domino's pizza truck when you were really drunk."

"Oh yeah," he smiles. "That was really fucking stupid... my dad had to pay a shitload to get me out of that one. I never heard the end of it." He rolls his eyes.

Like P.J. Jacobs, he comes from a family of

lawyers with connections, idle time, and plenty of money. His father probably sent a close friend to defend him and write a check. No big deal.

"Hey, can I buy you a beer?" His big hand touches my wrist.

"Sure." I shrug.

He waives at the bartender, "Hey Stanley, get this girl a... what are you drinking, Esme?"

"Ahm, Miller Light. Miller Light is fine." He reaches over the long oakwood bar, dipping his sleeve in a puddle of beer.

"Here you go, Esme. Cheers! It's nice to meet you." He hands me the brown bottle.

It's odd. We spent four years in college together at exactly same time. We went to the same bars, same restaurants, some of the same parties. My eyes followed him everywhere. He followed me nowhere. And here we were in Washington DC, meeting for the first time.

I see Melanie and Janey out of the corner of my left eye—they are whispering and giggling, covering their mouths. They know who he is, too.

We go on to talk—banal conversation, the details of which I cannot remember now. Which part of the city we lived in, where we worked, did I ever take that art class with that crazy professor MacFarland, and did I go to this party or that party at his frat house. He told me I was really funny. That I made him laugh.

As he spoke, he would touch my shoulder, then my wrist, and sometimes brush his fingers against mine.

I will always remember that moment outside in the rain at the divey bar with the cracked wood picnic tables. I felt airy and light, and maybe it was the beer, but for once, the words rolled effortlessly off my tongue. His eyes lit up when I answered any question, and then the recessed dimples would jump out from the corners of his mouth. I soaked it up. I wanted to stay here—in this moment—forever. He seemed to stand still, at that spot in front of the bar, for hours—abandoning his friends who had long since gone on to other pubs and parties. I noticed my friends had left, but I didn't care. I wanted to be nowhere else but here.

As I placed my empty beer on the top of the bar, he grabbed my left hand and wrapped it in his, holding it tightly with his coarse fingers, rough from years of pulling an oar on the crew team. I feel his oversized wristwatch slide down my fingers.

"Let's go," he said.

"Okay." I said effortlessly. I wanted to go everywhere with him.

He is drunk, yet I let him drive. I'm leaving with him, and I have just met him. I'm doing everything I know I'm not supposed to do. But I can't stop myself.

"Let's get something to eat." He drives fast. Navy blue BMW. Top down. The Washington monument on my left. New Order on the radio. He grabs the stick shift and then grabs my left hand and kisses it.

We pull into a trendy sports bar that he says he likes to go to on Thursday nights. I make a mental note. Because I'm sure we are going to start dating now. But eventually we'll break up, and I'll be stalking him here. Then I will be the psycho—not P.J. Jacobs.

Alex high fives the bartender and lots of other guys around the bar who obviously know him. I sit down quietly at a table in the back and light a cigarette. My smoking has gotten really out of control as of late, but I love it and do it anyway. It helps me not eat and calms my mind. I vow to run five miles tomorrow and repair my lungs.

He comes over to the table, grabs my cigarette out of my hand and takes a drag.

"You know, Esme. You're really are a cool chick."

I roll my eyes. If he only knew me. All the time on the sofa staring aimlessly at the ceiling. Pacing hard wood floors. He wouldn't like me if he knew. So I cover it up. I will be that girl.

"No, really. I mean you're super hot, but you're also really cool." He takes a drag taking me in, sizing me up.

My heart melts. I want to rip off his clothes. I have never had this kind of feeling—not even for my ex-boyfriend who I dated all through college and almost married. When we had sex, I watched CNN during the entire act because I more interested in what Manuel Noriega and the Contras were up to than getting off with him. Unlike most girls experimenting with everything, I wasn't that sexual in college. Actually I wondered if I was sexual period. I always worried that maybe my conservative mother had shut off that button in me.

"Hey. Hey." He motions for the bartender. "We'll have some... nachos." He looks at me for approval.

"Calamari? Good?"

"Yeah. Yeah. That's fine." I agree.

I become nervous as I often do when I know fattening food is about to be placed right in front of me. I know I will lose control and eat and then want to throw up right after. I know I will be laden with guilt all day tomorrow especially after I get on the scale. But tonight

I decide I do not care. I am going to eat *all* of this food with him. I'm not going to be the girl who diets.

The nachos arrive. We eat them rapidly like two starving children. I drip orange melted cheese down the front of my lavender sweater and try to wipe it off with a napkin with limited success.

He pays the bill with a platinum American Express card. He doesn't seem to care about money. He is in software sales and seems to be making a lot of it. He will later tell me that I'm too smart to be on the Hill—that I need to go make money and get a job in the private sector. The same thing my father has been telling me. I tell him I'm going to go to law school one day and that I want to make a difference in the world.

"Come on, let's get out of here." He grabs my hand.

I take his hand. I see why P.J. Jacobs wanted him so much, stayed with him so long despite probable extremely bad behavior. I can even see why she went psycho.

"So, where are we going?"

"My house…. I live right down the street." He opens the car door for me.

"Ahm, I think I should go home. I live on 18th— it's like 10 blocks that way." I know I'm not going home. But I also know I should protest a little bit.

"Come on. I want you to come over. Nothing's going to happen…. I promise." He shuts the car door.

"Right. Right." I smile at him with a skeptical look in my eyes. "I think I should just go home."

"Just come over for a little bit... then I'll drive you home… I want you to see our house."

He has a group house with three other guys who

had also attended his prep school. I know I shouldn't go in, but I want to go. I can't stop looking at him as he drives. I acquiesce.

He pulls into a winding gravel driveway, pushing the stick shift up and down, up and then down, and finally stops abruptly near the garage. He opens my door and takes my hand—helping me out like a perfect gentleman.

"Come on, don't worry! Nothing's going to happen. I'll take you home later." He grabs my hand.

I meet the three roommates who are shooting pool in the basement: Doug, Adam and David. They are in salmon pants and khaki shorts, and stripped polo shirts, so preppy and each so handsome. But no one looks like Alex.

"Hey, you guys. This is Esme.... We went to college together. Can you believe that?" He opens another beer.

They look up casually from their pool sticks. "Hey." They acknowledge my existence. Barely.

"Hi." I smile. I feel judged and nervous—like they are comparing me to P.J. Or some super model he has brought here before.

"Come on, let's go," he guides me up the dark brown and white-flecked carpeted basement stairs to the kitchen. He opens the refrigerator.

"Do you want anything? A beer?"

"No. No. I'm fine." I'm so wasted. I am having trouble focusing. Walking. I need another beer like I need a needle in my eyeball. Not that that hasn't stopped me before....

"Yeah, I'm good too."

He takes my hand right into his bedroom to the

left. There is an ivory white checked duvet on a bed perfectly made, white folded towels on a small white wooden shelf, and pictures of the Redskins and the Lincoln Memorial in his room. I look for the remnants of P.J.—maybe he has lied to me. But there are none. His room looks a hell of a lot better than mine.

"Hey," he pulls me in closely to his chest and kisses me. "I've been waiting to do this all night."

I say nothing. I won't become assertive or tell a man what I want until I'm halfway into my 30s. Right now, I'm a pacifist. As pliable as a rubber band.

He pushes me onto the bed. I know that I am too tired and too drunk to go home now. Plus, I can't resist him. He kisses my lips, my neck, the jutting bones around my neck, and then he pulls up my sweater covered with nacho cheese. Then he unhooks my bra, and sucks hard and long on my nipples. A little too hard. I push him away. He grabs my chin and kisses me passionately. I can't stop kissing him—my whole body tingles.

He gently pulls down my black leggings and pushes me down on the bed sliding his fingers between my legs. I tell myself that this is not going to happen. I remind myself that if I do in fact sleep with him tonight that he likely won't call me tomorrow, but I can't stop. His tongue is between my legs moving slowly, then rapidly and he has clasped my hands firmly to the sheets. I lean back feeling relaxed and alert at the same time. I don't ever remember feeling this type of sensation, and I just can't stop him from climbing on top and inside me. I have never really enjoyed sex that much nor had an orgasm from it. But this time it's different—I feel a deep and protracted release as I sigh out loud not even embarrassed. When we finish, he drapes his arm around my shoulders and kisses the top of my head softly.

"That was amazing," he whispers. "You are amazing."

And for once, I feel *amazing.*

He is gracious and kind in the morning—bringing me a tall bottle sparkling water and a cup of coffee— but I feel like hell. I know the mascara must be smeared down my eyes, and the hollows in my cheeks apparent. I just want to get home as soon as possible.

"I'll drive you home." He volunteers. Pulling another pair of khaki pants over his plaid boxer shorts. I lay in his bed staring at his hairy blonde chest, and concave stomach. He pushes his wavy hair back with water from the sink. I want him. I want him more than I have wanted anything ever, maybe even more than this job or my SAT score, but I lay there calmly. I say nothing.

"Ready?" He smiles.

I get dressed quickly so he doesn't see my body upright.

As he pulls up to my apartment building, literally ten blocks from his house, he leans over and kisses my neck three times.

"Hey. I had a great time last night. You're awesome. Can I have your number?"

I reach into my purse, push the cigarettes and lipstick to the side, and grab a pen and paper.

I write my number down.

"Cool. I'll call you." He pulls out of the driveway rapidly. I can hear the stones turning.

Famous last words is all I can think about and the familiar anxiety creeps back in. I will wait two days, then three days, and he won't call.

"Melanie! Melanie!" I rush into the apartment. Mascara smeared. Skin parched. I'm so thirsty.

"Hello?" She comes out of her bedroom, "Where in the hell have you been? Did you go home with Alex? And what the hell is all over your sweater?"

I look down and laugh. "Nachos. I think?"

"God," I throw myself onto the sofa, 'he is so fucking hot. I can't take it."

"Did you sleep with him, Esme?"

I smile sheepishly.

"I cannot believe you slept with him!" She exclaims.

"I couldn't help it! It just kind of happened."

"Unbelievable. Well, I knew you would."

"I think I'm in love with him." I whisper because I can't say it out loud. It's just two crazy.

"Good Lord, Esme. Alex Carrington? Really? He is such a meathead."

"I'm crazy about him. He's so hot. So funny." Well, he wasn't that funny actually. I'm not sure why I even said them.

He doesn't call on Sunday. I go back to work Monday and deal with the papers and the hearings, and the Congressman who throws pens at his staff. I try to bury myself in work. I have to put him out of my mind. This was a hook-up. A one-night thing. Let it go. Learn managed fucking care. I check my voicemail and again and again.

It's almost 4:00, and I'm hitting a wall. My phone at work is ringing. It's been ringing nonstop all day. Everyone wants to talk to me because everyone wants to talk to the Congressman.

I am irritated, tired of talking to all these allegedly important people. I grab the phone on the second ring.

"This is Esme." There is irritation in my voice.

"Hey Esme, how are you?" Breezy raspy voice.

"Who is this?"

"Who is this? Did you forget about me already?"

I recognize the voice.

"Alex?"

"Yeah. How are you?"

"Good. Busy... but good. How are you?"

"I'm great. You're busy there on Capitol Hill, huh? Trying to change the world?"

"Yeah. Actually, I am. Sorry. Not into selling software."

"Well, you can make a lot of money doing that. You'll never make any money at what you do."

"I'm fine now. Plus, I'm going to go to law school one day so I'll make money one day."

"I know you will. You're a bright girl."

"How do you know if I'm bright?"

"I can tell. I just know. Listen, I've got to go downtown to meet with a client. I was wondering if you wanted to meet for a drink."

I look at my outfit. Boring black pants suit. Average gold accessories. I am not prepared. But I want to see him. I would get on a fucking plane to Bangalore at this point to see him.

"I mean, do you have plans? I would love to see you."

"No, I was just going to go home and read a bunch of stuff for work."

"Fuck that. Come meet me. At Adobe Hotel. Do you know where that is? It's in Georgetown."

"Yeah. I think so."

"It's at 32rd and Wisconsin. It has an amazing view of the city on the rooftop deck."

21

"Okay."

"Okay. See you at 7:00 then, okay?"

"Okay."

I slam down the phone, grab my purse, and rush into the bathroom. Brush my teeth fastidiously. Take my hair out of the ponytail holder. Wipe the pretzel crumbs off of my jacket. Check my ass. Check it again. Put on lipstick. Fuck. I'm not prepared to see him.

I can't afford a cab, and I can't take the metro—it's nowhere near the hotel. So, I take off my heels, slip on my flip-flops, light a cigarette to assuage the anxiety and hoof it. I wipe my forehead over and over again with the Kleenex in my purse. It's so muggy here in the summer, and I can feel both my makeup and my nose running. I get on the elevator, ignore the annoying tourists, and hit the R for Rooftop.

As I get off, I turn my head left and right and then I see him in a corner table reading *The Wall Street Journal* and drinking a Vodka Tonic with lime—the sun beaming on his messy hair and slightly creased face. He looks up, sees me and smiles—waving at me.

He is perfect. As he always is.

Navy pinstriped suit. Lavender silk tie with tiny specks of white. Cufflinks. His eyes hidden by the green tinted Aviator sunglasses.

"Heyyyyy." He is mellow and light and everything I am not. He stands up. Grabs my shoulders and pulls them in closely to him and kisses my neck. "You smell good."

"Do you want a drink?" He holds up his glass of vodka, ice cubes half melted now. "Or should we get a bottle of wine?'

"I think I want a glass of wine.... Vodka makes me wasted." I am not good with hard alcohol. I love vodka, but it makes me crazy. And I don't feel like being crazy right now. I don't want to blow this moment.

"Well," he laughs, pulling off his sunglasses and setting them on the glass table gently, "maybe I should get you a Vodka Tonic then."

He gets the wine list and scours it. He knows the grapes, the years and brands.

"You like Silver Oak?" He looks up at me. "Cabernet?

"Yes. Sure." I nod and clench my jaw. I don't even know what that is. I know nothing about wine except that I love it and can't really afford it, except out of a box.

We go on to drink the wine. I gulp mine fast. I notice that I'm a glass ahead of him at all times, and I am not eating much of the sliders and artichoke dip he has ordered.

For years, I have managed to live on pretzels, black beans, and rice. As I watch him eat chip after chip, I wonder how he stays so fit. So lined and chiseled and angular. He eats unabashedly—no worries, no guilt. I decide to start eating some chips. I don't want him to think I'm one of those girls who only orders salads.

"Look at that, Esme," he points to The Washington Monument, then the Capitol, then the Jefferson Memorial. "Isn't this a great view? You can see everything here. Here you are. The center of all the power in the world."

From this rooftop table, you can see everything magnificent about D.C. And the sky is now salmon pink with blended lines of pale blue emanating out of the falling sun. It feels magical now.

23

"I know it's amazing." I lean out over the balcony almost falling.

I turn to him.

"Do you like power? "

"Do you?" He leans back in the round pine green leather chair.

"I don't know. I've never had it before. "

" But you have it now." He wipes his forehead beading up with sweat with a white stained napkin.

"No, I don't!" I roll my eyes.

"Yeah, you do. Look at all those people who call you every day… who just want a piece of you…." He squeezes my hand. "I can't blame them. I would want a piece of you too."

"They want a piece of my boss! He has the power. Not me."

"But, you kind of have it too—because they have to get to you—to get to him."

"Well, you have power…. In what you do."

"How?" He lights up a Marlboro Red. "I'm just a sales guy."

"Because you are good at what you do, and you make money. And money is power."

"No, no, money can bring power. I mean eventually. But money isn't power. They are something totally different."

"Which do you want?" I press my chin against my hand and lean in to the table.

"Whatever you want me to have."

He laughs and squeezes my hand.

"You are so beautiful, do you know that?"

"Seriously, which do you want?"

"Money…. Of course."

He came from money. And he's going to keep it.

We go on to talk about work and he tells me about customer relations management software and their customers. I tell him I'm trying to write a bill that will help uninsured people have access to affordable health care. We talk about P.J. a little—how she calls him incessantly and shows up randomly in bars that he frequents. He tells me he will protect me from her—but that he hopes that she doesn't show up when we're together somewhere. I feel my chest rise, and take in a deep breath.

He's talking about us in the future tense.

"You know. You have to come to our beach house. Why don't you come this weekend? Bring some of your friends…."

Bathing suit. I freak out in my mind. I'm not ready for that.

"Well…. Maybe."

"Why not?" He lights another cigarette.

"Well," I light a cigarette anxiously.

"Because I'm not really in good shape now. I need to lose five pounds… then I'll come."

I immediately want to take the words back. Rewind. I want to be the confident girl who eats French Fries with ease not the girl who talks about her weight. Fuck.

"Oh come on, stop. You have a great body. You're so thin. Come on… just come. It will be fun."

I gulp my wine. I suggest we get another bottle. He agrees and orders it. I'm getting tipsy. I become looser. I like *that* girl. And I want that girl here.

"Hey, where do you want to go tonight? Why don't you just stay at my place?"

"Nooooo," I pause. "I have to be at work early tomorrow."

"So? We'll get up early, and I'll drive you home."

"Why don't we just stay here tonight?"

"Here?"

"Yeah. Why not? It will be fun."

I am now whimsical and fun. I am someone else.

"You're serious?"

"Yeah. Why not? It's a beautiful night. A beautiful hotel ... and life is short."

The hotel has to be $300 to $400 dollars a night, but I don't care. I'll put it on my credit card. I want to stay.

"Okay, let's do it." He laughs, leans back in his chair and throws down the platinum Am Ex, signs our bill. Gets a key.

We get to our room on the fourth floor. He opens the door, and pushes me onto bed.

"God, I want you." He kisses my neck and then my lips, and then places his tongue on mine. He unbuttons my snug suit jacket, my bra, and his mouth is on my breasts, and I want him. I undo his tie; he throws off his jacket, pulling down my pants, grabbing my ass. It happens this fast. It's animalistic. He turns me over kissing my back. Holding my ass tightly.

"You have a great ass. You know that."

I am nervous. I don't feel like my ass is firm enough yet. I just wish I had had two more months to do more lunges.

I turn over, undo his buckle, pull down his boxers. Everything on his body is perfect and how it should be. I touch his stomach—it is lengthy and lined, hairy and flat. I think about my hips, my saddlebags, and I feel a bit inadequate. But, we go on. We have sex three times that night.

As he kisses my stomach in the morning, his tongue on my belly button, he says, "Wow. That was amazing."

I am amazing.

"I know. I know."

I hold his tousled hair in my hands and he keeps kissing my stomach. I feel like finally I know what desire is—how it feels to want someone that much.

"Come to the beach this weekend." He rolls over facing me.

"Okay," I capitulate. "Hey, what time is it?"

"Eight. Fuck. It's 8:00!" He jumps up. I jump up.

"Oh my God. I have to be at work at 8:30."

"Fuck!" He stands up, sliding on his blue oxford cloth boxers, and I can't help but stare at him while he dresses even though I'm very much panicked about work. I just started this job, and I don't want to blow it.

I pull on my black silk underwear—reaching across the bed for my bra.

"Listen, I don't have time to go home. I'm just going to have to go to work from here."

"Are you kidding? You're going to go to work in the same clothes?" He laughs.

"Yes," I rush into the bathroom, washing old makeup and smeared mascara off my face.

"I have a toothbrush. I just have to go. I can't be late."

He laughs.

"You're insane."

"I know. But I have to be there. I don't want to get in trouble my first week. I'll just run home at lunch and change."

"Okay," He pushes his body against me as I bend over the sink and rubs his hands in the running water and then through his curly hair.

So, he drops me off in front of my building. I press my clothes down, ironing out the wrinkles and pull my hair into a bun.

"You're crazy, you know that." He kisses me. "So, I'll call you later. But you're coming to the beach."

"Okay. I've got to go." I kiss his cheek and rush up the front marble steps and then another five flights to my office.

Today I walk in through the back door to avoid the Congressman's office. I calmly and nonchalantly walk through the office and sit down at my desk and open the paper. I'm so hung-over that the words are blurry. I tell myself that I have to focus.

"Abbe, who has been warming up to me a bit, looks up from her desk, her boxy glasses sliding down her nose.

"Aren't those the same clothes you had on yesterday?"

"Yes." I confess.

"Really?"

"Yes."

"So, were you out all night then?"

"Yes."

"With that boy?" I had confided in her about how crazy I was about Alex. She knows everything.

"Yes, with him."

I think she is going to send me home to change and give me a lecture about professionalism.

"Good for you." She smiles and goes back to typing her speech.

Wow. She's a lot cooler than I thought.

After the hearing that day, I call Melanie and confess. I realize she must be worried about me.

"Ah, hello Houdini? Where the hell have you been?" She sounds angry.

I tell her about having dinner with Alex and then spending the night at the hotel. I tell her the sex was amazing, and I think I'm in love with him and that we have to go the beach that weekend. Melanie has never been to the beaches in Delaware, and she is all about the party. She is on board and is going to round up Jane.

Alex doesn't call me the next day, which causes me a great deal of anxiety. I constantly check the red light that blinks on the phone on my desk, but it's never him.

I wonder if he still wants me to go the beach after all. Why hasn't he called?

Then, suddenly, two days later, the phone rings, and it is him.

"Hey, so you guys are coming to the beach this weekend, right?"

"Yeah. We're gonna leave Friday after work, I think."

"Okay cool. We'll be there. We're leaving at noon, so just come whenever."

"Okay. I'll have to work till 5:00 though."

"That's fine. No worries."

"Okay."

"Okay. See you there."

There is a pit in my stomach when I hang up. I walk outside to have a cigarette. I feel like I'm already losing him. I feel like how P.J. must have felt. *He is*

29

making me crazy. First he wants me and thinks I'm amazing. Now he seems to be detaching. I don't know how to act. I start to obsess.

The same toxic thoughts that always run through my brain late at night have invaded it during the day. I have to shut it down.

I decide to go to beach... put these thoughts out of my mind.

On Friday Melanie, Jane and I load up the beach towels and sunscreen and beer in Mel's convertible and head to the beach. We finally arrive at 8:00, but when we walk in, Alex is not there nor are any of his housemates. We throw our bags in the living room, but I have no idea where it is we are supposed to be.

There is a note on the countertop.

"Esme, we're at FishHead's, come meet us. A."

I slip on a blood orange strapless sundress and pull my hair back in a high ponytail; it so humid here.

When we arrive, Alex is sitting at a wooden table with the prep school friends. Tan long arms moving up and down with green bottled beers and shot glasses. Melanie and Jane gravitate toward them within minutes of our arrival—they are already flirting. Alex, however, can barely stand up. He's totally hammered.

"Hey, what do you girls want? Three Vodka Cranberries for these girls."

He slaps down the credit card.

"Open a tab. Carrington!"

He was always a guy to spend a lot of money. He was really quite generous—especially considering I had about $20 left in my checking account.

"You are so hot, you know that?"

He pulls me into him, white button down oxford

untucked, five o'clock shadow, greasy, salty hair. Even while sloppy drunk, he is still the most handsome man I have ever seen. His eyes are the exact color of the ocean we are now facing.

We go on to drink many more Vodka Cranberries. Alex's friend Dave walks us home, and we all go into separate rooms.

Alex can barely stand up. He crashes on the bed, and I stand in the hallway peering in. I have no idea what to do. And then, just like that, he gets up and pulls my arm in toward him.

"Come on baby... come sleep in here."

But the sex isn't so good this time. The romance is absent. He is covered in sand and really drunk. But I stay with him and convince myself that tonight is just an aberration. Tomorrow he'll be back to the way he was—he'll tell me how amazing I am and how happy he is that I am here.

But when I wake up, he is already up, pulling on his army green cargo shorts, rubbing his hands through his curly hair with splashed water in the bathroom.

"Hey." He sees me open my eyes.

"Hey." I smile. He sits down on the edge of the bed, and rubs my head. As he sits there placidly, looking down at me, I stare at his stomach one ripple after the next. I have never even seen him exercise.

"Hey," I pull his hand toward me. "What are you doing? Come lay with me." I want him to come back and lay with me, just a little bit longer, but he has to go now.

"I've got to go, " He kisses my forehead. "Cal is waiting on me." He slips a white T-shirt with his fraternity letters across the top.

I look at the clock. It's 10:00.

31

"Where are you going?" I sit up.

"Oh, we're just going to Ellie's for brunch—and then we'll probably hit the beach. We'll catch up with you guys later."

I stare at him blanky. Am I not invited to breakfast? But before I can ask, he is gone.

He is gone then... he is gone all day. I find Jane and Melanie, and we head to the beach and read magazines and talk about Alex and his friends all day. Where they are, why they didn't invite us. Whether we should go try to find them.

As it approaches 4:00, we pack up our beach bags and gather our belongings. I slip on my pale blue baseball hat and throw on a pair of baggy shorts. My black bikini top with the wire underneath creates the illusion of cleavage. My stomach is flat, but not flat enough, and I search fervently for a T-shirt in my bag but can't find one.

As we approach the boardwalk and begin our ascent home, we run right into them. I see Alex approaching me—same cargo shorts, no shirt, green-tinted Aviator sunglasses.

"Hey..." He puts his arm around me. Breezy. Light. Just like the sea wind that is blowing my hair everywhere. My baseball cap flies off.

"Esme, this is Cal, another guy I went to high school with."

I shake his hand and introduce him to my friends. I am irritated but trying to be pleasant.

"Why don't you guys head back with us? We'll shower. Grill some burgers."

"Thanks, Alex. I mean where did you think we were going to go?

It just comes out of my mouth. Just like that. I can't suppress my agitation.

"Esme, come on, relax. I just thought you'd come *with us.*"

"Oh, well thank you so much." I grab my beach bag and start to walk away. My friends stand there. It is uncomfortable and tense, and it's just too hot to fight.

"What's your problem?" He grabs my elbow firmly as I attempt to walk away.

"Nothing." I pull back.

"Why are you acting like this?" He raises his voice.

"Well, I mean you blow us off all day, and then you show up at like 5:00, and tell us we can now come home with you and grab showers. How magnanimous of you."

"Why are you acting like this? Listen, I told you Cal was coming down. And I told you to bring your friends with you, and we'd all catch up later."

"Fine. Let's go."

That night I try to shake it off and get rid of the rage that I suspect will resurface after the consumption of several Vodka Cranberries. I somehow keep the anger suppressed. I don't want to ruin the weekend for my friends, and I don't want to fight with Alex.

That night he is the life of the party. At the bar, he makes friends, asks me what I need, what my friends need. Buys us Vodka Cranberries. Kisses my cheek every so often—usually after a shot of Yagermeister or Petrone.

And the summer goes on—just like this. I come to the beach house, some weekends, and only on his terms. He is absent during the vast majority of most days—and with me only at night.

When we go back to D.C., he'll wait several days before calling me.

I don't ask questions or try to get more from him. I accept it and throw myself into my work.

But as summer turns into fall, I wonder what I'm doing. My friends tell me I'm wasting my time, that he is never going to be my boyfriend—let alone a good boyfriend. But I still see him the way I did in college—everywhere and filling up every space. I still remember, the first night, lying in his bed kissing him under those starchy white cotton sheets, wanting it to never end.

Alex is also working all the time—always closing a deal, and then when the deal closes, he goes out with his friends to celebrate. Sometimes he asks me to come, and when he does, I always do. But a lot of the time he goes without me. I wonder if he sees P.J. when I'm not around—if he's seeing someone else. The thought of it actually takes over my mind when I'm at hearings, and I find myself obsessing over the girl he could be with right now.

Then, one day, I wake up, rush out to my car to go to work, and my car is gone. The landlord, I discover, had it towed because I inadvertently parked it in the wrong spot. I start to panic. I don't know where it is or how to get it. I'm going to be late for work. I don't think I have $100 in my checking account to pay for it. I don't know what to do or who to call. I don't even have that many friends here.

I vacillate. But then I call Alex.

I'm convinced he is going to yell at me, tell me

he's busy, in the middle of a deal, how could I be so stupid... but he's nothing but soothing and kind.

"It's okay. I know where your car is. I'll be over in a few. You're at home, right?"

"Yeah." I'm crying but trying to rub the mascara off my face. I stand there on the overgrown green grass, long khaki skirt and pale pink oversize polo shirt, my hair in a ponytail with a pink ribbon. Just waiting.

And then he pulls up in the navy blue BMW with the rooftop down. Dressed perfectly in a pale blue seersucker suit with a lemon yellow tie.

"Hey," he wipes my eye. "Don't cry... it's fine. We'll get it."

And just like that, he drives me to the sketchy place where my car resides. He hands the attendant $100 and tells me to follow him back home. He is calm and gracious, and he just kind of amazes me.

It is times like this that I fall in love with him all over again.

But he doesn't call me later. In fact, he doesn't call me for about five days. The novelty of me is clearly waning.

I am no longer something new. I am like P.J. Old. Boring.

Melanie tries to help. She introduces me to a friend of her boyfriend, and I try to move on, date other people, but I don't really like him.

I just come home from work exhausted, feeling more miserable and missing Alex all the more. I read *The New Yorker* and spend my weekends alone with books and movies.

By October, we have officially stopped dating. He has just disappeared. However, I have stabilized and met some new girls at work and am spending my evenings at the gym or reading fiction to escape my life.

At least I'm not obsessing over *him* anymore.

Then, one day, while at work, red felt pen in hand editing a speech, concentrating on each word and how it is placed, my phone rings. It is him.

"Hey. How are you girl?"

"Good. Busy, but good. And you?" Be casual. Detached.

"Hey, I'm great. It's so good to hear your voice."

"Yeah. It's good to hear your voice too." I tap my pen impatiently. Thinking about the cigarettes in my purse.

"Listen, I have to tell you something."

My heart drops. He's getting married. He's back with P.J. He's having a baby. The parade of horribles goes through my mind...

"I'm moving ... to New York."

Moving? Moving? Oh my God. This is far worse than I imagined. Even though I haven't seen him in some time, Alex is my anchor. He's the one person I really know here besides Melanie. He is my college, my past, a time when I was really happy and fulfilled.

"What?"

"Yeah.... I'm going to New York."

"Why? I mean you love D.C. ... you grew up here. What about your job?"

"Well, I'm kind of over D.C. It's pretty lame. And I got this great opportunity... to go into investment banking. There's tons of money in it, and it's a great firm."

"Investment banking? What about your software company?"

"No money, Esme. No money. Banking is where it's at .... "

"When do you leave?"

"In two weeks."

"Two weeks?? I can't believe this.

"I just wanted you to know.... and Doug may have a going away party or something. I'll let you know."

That casual. That cavalier. I just wanted you to know....

"And listen, if you are *ever* in New York, I want you to call me okay? You always have a place to stay."

And that is it. We hang up.

As the fall progresses, I stop at the red light, I lean my head against the pane of my left window aimlessly, watching all those maize and pumpkin orange leaves scatter through gusting winds on the path of Rocky Creek parkway, and I find myself thinking about Alex again—and what he is doing and where he is living, if he likes New York City.

But I've been thinking about him a lot less now, which is a relief. I haven't found a new boyfriend to replace him. I guess that I am the girl that I always said I would never be—the girl that always has to have a boyfriend to fill up the space

But I am trying to embrace the ambiguity my life now holds and not pressure myself—to fill out law school applications or apply for a new higher paying job.

I try to do a good job at work. I go in on the weekends and write letters and edit speeches. During recess, I fly to the district office to meet with constituents. I run for miles and miles up Rockcreek Parkway on the weekends. I run until my hamstrings burn, and my heart beats out of my chest.

And the time seems to pass with relative ease. And the sadness seems to be lifting.

Then one October day, as I'm sifting through the piles of mail on my desk, I find an invitation to a conference in New York City—it's a topic I'm very interested in, so I call the sponsor immediately. They tell me my conference fee will be waived because I work for the government, and when I approach Abbe cautiously with the request, she approves it. So I'm going to New York City, and of course, I think of Alex. And his standing offer. I just have to see him.

I decide to call him. Roll into voicemail.

"Hey there, how are you? I hope you are well. Hey, I'm coming to New York on the third for a conference. Maybe we can get together."

He immediately calls me back. Hmm. The market must be slow today—I figured he'd be on the trading floor of the New York Stock Exchange making the deals he is so fond of.

"Hey you. New York is great. Of course, I would love to see you. You can stay here. Where is your conference? Okay. Here's my new number."

Stay with him? Of course, I want to stay with him. I immediately call Melanie with the news.

"Whatever. You are just hell bent on this. I hope you get your wonder fuck." She hangs up the phone.

I leave him a voicemail with the details of my trip. He tells me to meet him after at his office on Wall Street—which just happens to be very close to my conference is being held. When I get on the train from

DC to New York, my mind races. I think about seeing him, eating dinner with him, kissing him, what his apartment will look like, how it will be when we see each other again. I try to read my *The Wall Street Journal* so we have things to discuss, but I just can't focus.

I dress as best as I can. I want to look perfect. Heather gray sleeveless dress, high grey suede pumps to match. I even wear gray eyeliner, silver jewelry and carry a gray leather clutch. I'm totally broke from this outfit, but I know it will be worth it.

When I get to New York, it is incredibly hot—a scorching fall day, and I feel like I'm going to suffocate in the subway. There is no air conditioning, and people are pushing me into the silver bar I'm holding on to.

I hate it here. It's so crowded and dirty; I can feel the makeup melting down my face, and the sweat trickling down my bra. And I have all day to go before I see him.

The conference is long and boring. I keep staring at my watch... four more hours to go. I excuse myself when the cheesecake is brought out at lunch and sneak out to have a cigarette. At 5:00, I call Alex at work. He picks up immediately.

"I'll be done at 5:30 then. Do you want me to just come there?"

"Yes. It's off Gold Street. Tall silver building. Everson Investments. Tenth floor."

"Okay, see you then."

"Okay, babe." He replies.

I smile. Just like old times... he called me babe.

I rush to the bathroom and clean up and douse

myself with perfume. I want him to want me back. I want him to want me the way he did when we first met.

I walk outside and hail a cab like a confident New Yorker and guide the driver to my destination.

"Yes... right there. That tall silver building... right there." I rush out of the cab and walk into the building and hop on the elevator.

The elevator opens up into a grand gold lobby with tall glass windows, high ceilings, spiral staircase. A beautiful woman in pink suit sits at a long walnut desk with a headphone on her ear and smiles at me.

"Hello," she pulls the headpiece down from her mouth, "Can I help you?"

She's probably sleeping with him. She's stunning—smooth milky skin, no lines, brown saucer eyes, straight caramel hair pulled back loosely in a bun. I'm immediately suspicious.

"Yes. I'm here to see Alex Carrington."

" One minute, please." She returns to the phone.

"Alex, you have a guest downstairs."

And minutes later, he slides down the walnut wood spiral staircase—first his black wingtip shoe, then down another stair, the ankle of his navy blue pin-striped suit, then his long leg, the top of the jacket, see the cufflinks on the white shirt as his left arm grabs the railing, and then his pink striped tie, few more stairs and he is at the bottom facing me. He waves, and I smile and wave back.

"Hey you." I inch toward him. "Hey, welcome to New York." He pulls me into him, hugs me tightly and kisses my cheek.

"Jackie, did you meet Esme?"

"Yes, hello." The beautiful receptionist stands up and shakes my hand.

"Esme and I went to college together." He puts his arm around my shoulder and pauses.

"We're old friends."

Old friends? I feel my heart drop.

"She is here visiting... from DC."

"D.C.??" She stares at me.

It's as if I said I was from Iowa. Suddenly, D.C. seems so pedestrian. Everything seems so much cooler in New York. This is a real city not a town like DC.

"Yes, I live in D.C. I'm just here for a conference."

"I see.... Well, welcome to New York."

"Come on. I'll take you on a tour of the office," He grabs my hand.

"Let's go upstairs." It feels so good to hold his hand again.

He guides me upstairs and introduces me to his colleagues—all young and attractive and well dressed. He never lets go of me—holds my elbow, pulls me around the floor. He's almost acting like I'm his girlfriend. I meet more people; look at the televisions he shows me with quotes on ticker tape from NASDAQ and NYSE.

"Can we get out of here?" I whisper to him. "I just want to change. I'm so hot."

"Yeah, yeah, just give me a minute." He walks off to his office to grab his leather satchel with *The Wall Street Journal* and analyst reports peeking out— buy, hold, sell. Stuff I don't understand or really care about.

His colleagues stare at me. I smile and look

41

around the room at the TVs blaring news about the markets—I feign enthusiasm.

The fashionable lithe girls size me up. They look at my shoes, my calves and my stomach. I glare back at them confidently. I've been eating apples and lettuce for a week.

"Hey, ready?"

"Yeah, I'm ready."

He puts his arm on my shoulder. "Night guys, see you tomorrow."

As we exit, I feel like I'm going to pass out again. There are no trees in New York—there is no respite from this heat and all these people. I walk ahead of him. He takes my luggage, and I hail a cab.

"Wait. Wait. What are you doing?" He grabs my elbow.

"I'm getting a cab. What?"

"Esme, we're in New York now. Not D.C."

"So?" I don't understand.

"Cabs are really expensive here. We're gonna take the subway."

He has to be kidding me. We're going to lug this suitcase onto the subway? I can't bear the thought of getting back into that sauna.

"Can't we just take a cab? It's so hot. And I have all this crap."

"Esme," He is firm now, almost paternalistic, "We're taking the subway. This is New York. It's very expensive. Come on."

I can't believe it. Money never ever mattered in D.C. Now we can't even take a cab?

So we take the subway. We get off somewhere in the West Village.

He wheels my bag and pulls his satchel over his other shoulder.

"Listen, I don't have my own place yet. It won't be ready for another couple weeks. So, I'm crashing with Brett, a friend of mine from high school."

He just now tells me this? That he is residing on the sofa of a one-bedroom apartment?

"Really? Well, are you sure it's okay if I stay there?"

"Yeah. Yeah. I mean Brett won't be home. He always works late. We barely see each other."

We get there. It's a walk up. We walk up four flights of heavy wooden stairs. I think I'm going to collapse. He unlocks the door. There are big tall warehouse windows, but as I look to the left, I see Alex's golf clubs, a suit hanging on top of his golf clubs, a small black and white kitchen with dishes everywhere, and clothes and baseball mitts scattered on the floor. This is the opposite of his pristine bedroom in DC.

"Here." He drops my luggage in the middle of the living room. "We'll put your stuff here for now."

He plunges on the dirty beige velour sofa, spreads his legs, unfastens his tie.

"Can I use your bathroom?" I have to wash my hands. My face. I'm sweating so much that I decide I need a shower.

"Is it okay if I take a shower and change?"

"Yeah, sure." He tosses his white crisp cotton shirt on the orange round antique chair, and opens a Beck's beer. "You want one?"

"Yeah, sure."

I take the cold beer with me into the cold shower.

The water pounds on my neck and shoulders, and I take fast sips and start to become glued again. There are stains on the white bathtub tile and there is nothing but a razor, Head and Shoulders shampoo and Ivory soap in the shower. I rub the soap in my hands over and over before I use it—trying to get their germs off first.

But, as I shut off the water and dry myself off with a crusty blue hard towel, I feel better. I slide on a khaki mini skirt and a J. Crew navy top and flat sandals.

But when I come out of the bathroom, the roommate, Brett is there. He is a towhead blonde, short, stocky, and fucking hyper.

"Hey, hey, you're Esme, right?" He blazes down the small hallway, grabs my hand that I just washed several times.

"Yes. Hello."

"Hey, I'm Brett…nice to meet you. Alex and I grew up together."

He is pacing up and down the hallway runner, and his eyes are red. I immediately think he has to be on coke.

"So Alex is crashing here now. And you guys are welcome to stay here. Alex has a pullout in the living room."

"Yeah, thanks. I'll be leaving really early tomorrow." I push an errant hair behind my ear. This is not what I expected. Brett lights a cigarette. Thank God.

"Can I have one of those?"

"Yeah, yeah sure." He paces, looking for matches, find them, lights up a Camel and hands it to me.

They break off into conversation—about the Yankees, stocks and bonds.

I tune out, smoke the cigarette and feel relief, walk around the apartment and look at the books lined up in a white oak bookshelf.... Salman Rushie, J.D. Salinger, John Updike, John Irving. I'm impressed. I reach for *Franny and Zoey* and feel Brett staring at me.

"Sorry. I didn't mean to go through your stuff. This is such a great book though. Have you read it?"

"Are you kidding? Of course I read it. I did my freshman year paper on it."

Alex is smoking and looking out the window at something. He doesn't seem interested.

"I love J.D Salinger." I hug the book into my chest, almost instinctively.

"Me too. Did you read *Raise High the Roof Bea*m?

" Yes. I loved it."

"Me too. God. What a book." He drags his cigarette one more time and then rushes for the ashtray to put it out—then brings me the ashtray. He is fucking manic but at least interesting.

"You ready?" Alex puts out his cigarette. "Let's go get something to eat."

"Yeah, I'm starving. Let's go."

"Where you guys going?" Manic lights up another cigarette off of his first.

"I don't know. Probably SoHo. You wanna meet up with us later? I'll call you."

"Okay, cool. Yeah. Maybe I will."

Brett keeps staring at me intently and is making me nervous. This is not turning out like I thought it would.

45

And Alex is definitely different.

"Come on." He grabs my arm so firmly that it hurts. I pull away. "Come on." He grabs it again. "Let's go."

"I don't want to get back on the subway. Can we just walk please?"

"Wow. I didn't know you were such a little princess."

"I'm not Alex. I'm just tired, and it's so hot in the subway. I'd rather walk."

"Yeah, that's fine." He lights up a cigarette and walks faster. I struggle to keep up.

"What do you want to eat? What are you in the mood for?" He looks back at me.

"I don't know. Maybe fish, something light.... "

"I kinda want a steak. I'm starving." He walks faster down Houston Street. I wonder why he even bothered to ask.

"That's fine. I mean it's your city—wherever."

As we approach Grand Street, he stops.

"Oh, let's go here. I love this place. It's really cool. And they usually have a DJ who spins records."

It is a small bar in SoHo with a very small restaurant adjacent to it.

We sit down at the wide stainless steel bar. A bartender with a red T-shirt, goatee, and tattoos on his forearms, approaches us. I look around. Everyone is smoking, talking, hands moving effusively. There is an energy here, and I can't help but get sucked into it.

"What do you want? Vodka Tonic?" Alex grabs the menu and starts skimming the entrees.

"No. Vodka Cranberry."

He orders two drinks and stares at the menu. He

doesn't ask me about my day or my work. Doesn't tell me I'm beautiful or how glad he is that I am here.

"Do you know what you want?" He asks me impatiently. He seems eager to order.

The drinks arrive. I grab a small straw and begin slurping it.

I haven't even looked at the menu yet. I pick one up.

"I'll probably just get the pasta with pesto."

"I think I'm going to get the lamb…. Why don't you try the lamb? It's really good here."

"I don't really eat meat."

"Really? Why not? What's up with that?"

"I don't know. I just don't like it. It's a texture thing… "

"That's weird, Esme. You could use a little meat on your bones." He slams the menu down on the bar and looks around fervently.

Suddenly, Brett arrives. How did he even know we were here? He runs up to Alex and slaps his back. Alex is now animated. Alive. Full of smiles. As if I was the albatross around his neck pulling him down into a sinking sea, and Brett was the life preserver sent here at this moment to rescue him.

"Hey Man, sit down, we were just going to order."

I cannot fucking believe this. I'm now on a date with Alex *and Brett.* And I'm sleeping at Brett's with Alex.

We sit at the bar—the three of us—they order a lot of Corona's and shots. I have more Vodka Cranberries. This not the perfect night—I expected—not even close.

When the food arrives, I slowly pick at the pasta while they reminisce about high school and football and crew. Brett finally begins to include me in the conversation, leans forward, and asks me how we met. He seems to be flirting with me, kind of, and Alex doesn't seem to be at all jealous.

As it approaches 11:00 or so, and we are all now sufficiently wasted, the waitress drops off the check.

Alex drops the platinum Am Ex. As he always does.

"We don't take credit cards. Only cash."

"Fuck," he ruffles through his wallet. "I only have five bucks."

"I don't have any cash either…. Brett goes through his. "You really don't take credit cards?"

"No." The waitress is annoyed as if we should have known.

Alex turns to me. I shuffle through my unorganized purse of lipsticks, receipts, pens, mace…. I open my wallet. I thought I spent my last ten bucks on that cab to his office, but I find a lot of money. I forgot. I took out a bunch before I came, just in case. I guess this is that just in case.

"Yeah, I have cash." I hand him all of it. $150. The bill is $130. I have had a horrible night, and now I'm paying for the company of two men who I don't even want to be with.

"Esme, thanks, " Brett leans over. "I'll get you some cash. We'll pay you back."

They don't. Alex is cheap now. And has metamorphosized into some dickface New Yorker.

Brett finally leaves. He says he is going to give us some time alone, which I no longer covet.

Alex and I go to a wine bar for a glass of Bordeaux. I say little. Then he probes and probes. I tell him how he has changed, how I feel like he doesn't even want me here—that he would prefer to hang out with Brett. We get into a fight, and he tells me I'm spoiled again. Until finally, he apologizes and tells me he is sorry and glad I am here and how beautiful I look. He rubs my hand and pulls it to his lips. Suddenly, I feel amazing again.

After a couple of drinks we go back to Brett's little apartment. Manic is asleep, and I am grateful for that. The last thing I want is to watch Alex engage in more frat boy chitchat with Brett. I excuse myself, go to the bathroom, and slip on the short white cotton Laura Ashley nightgown that I wore all through college when I slept at my nice, normal boyfriend's house. I think about calling him, telling him I fucked up, that I made a mistake leaving. But I stop myself. I don't want to hurt him anymore than I have, and I know, that in the end, something was always missing between us.

I climb onto the sofa and hug my knees. I don't get into the daybed where he lies flat on his back in his rose oxford cloth boxers. I stare at him and his surfboard stomach; a part of me wants him so badly, and a part of me just hates him. I pull the navy fleece blanket over my legs, I turn to the side facing him. "Hey," he says, his thumb rubbing my lips and then my cheek, "what are you doing? Come lay with me."

I lay there still, corpselike, staring blankly into his eyes. I feel tipsy and also sad. Sad for what we had that is gone, sad for who he is now, and for a night absent of everything I wanted it to be.

"Come here; come lay with me." He pulls me down on to the bed. Starts kissing my neck, and rubbing the back of my leg. "You are so muscular ….. God, you have a great ass."

And he pulls me in—the lines, the charm, the chest hair against my back. It all comes back.

I don't really remember the sex that night, what I do remember is the sex that next morning. He lifts my thin white nightgown, and grabs the back of my legs. He is aggressive, and I am pissed off but obedient. I still want every part of him. He is in me so deeply—it almost hurts—but I want him to go farther—I want him to be as inside of me as one can be.

The sun is beating through the tall warehouse windows hitting my face, and I open my eyes, and close them. My head is pounding, and I'm so thirsty. The alarm goes off—it's 7:00. We were supposed to be up at 6:00. Brett is gone. I now remember hearing the door slam as he left for work.

"Fuck," Alex rolls to the other side. "God, I don't want to get up. It's 7:00. Fuck. We have to get going. What time is your train?"

"Nine."

"Okay, you shower first. Then I'll go, and you can lock up before you leave."

We do not cuddle. We do not embrace. He does not bring me bottled water.

It is as if nothing has happened, and I am invisible now—lying right next to him. I slip my nightgown over my head and shower quickly; freezing water that I cannot adjust, beating on my head. I dry off rapidly and slip my nightgown back on. My clothes are in the living room. I towel dry my hair which is now curly and frizzy. When I walk into the living room, he jumps up and rushes into the shower.

And, I sit there, on the pale pine wooden floors with nicks and stains, I hug my knees closely in.

Wondering why I am here, what I am doing—maybe I just can't grow up, maybe I just want to recreate college or create it the way I always wanted it to be. I feel that familiar feeling—spilling over me like a rushing tidal wave, enveloping me in black; my heart sinks hitting the wooden floor. I hug my knees tighter, press my forehead against my kneecaps, drops from my wet hair hitting the wood floor.

Alex comes to the living room, waist swaddled in a long white terry cloth towel.

"Esme, what are you doing?"

I say nothing. I feel like I'm on the verge of losing it.

"Come on. You have to get ready. I *have* to go to work."

Suddenly, I realize all my cash is gone — we spent it last night. And I have to get to Penn Station to catch the train home. I ruffle through my purse—quarters, pennies, no dollars. Open my wallet, search for my blue debit card. It's gone. I can't find it anywhere. Dump my purse on the floor.

"What are you doing?" He pulls his towel off and rubs it through his hair.

"I don't have any cash… and I can't find my debit card."

"What do you mean you can't find it?"

"I can't find it. I don't know. And I gave you all my cash last night… can you just give me ten bucks for a cab?"

"You don't have any money?"

"No." I shuffle through my purse.

"God, Esme…." He paces fervently. "I've got to get out of here…" He walks over to a tall jar of

51

change. He starts to dump it out. Slides quarters and nickels at me across the floor.

"I gave you all my money! I don't want your fucking change!"

"Listen, I'm in a rush. I can't believe you have no money at all."

"I GAVE IT ALL TO YOU LAST NIGHT!"

"You are spoiled. You know, that? I'm not your doctor Daddy... I can't take care of you anymore."

"Fuck you." I storm out of the room and into the bathroom.

"Come here! Come here! Esme ... "

"NO. Leave me alone!" I slam the bathroom door. The tears start to pour. I am so angry that I contemplate breaking the glass jars holding cotton swabs on the floor. Shattering glass everywhere. Hoping he steps on each sharp shard, and it cuts both of his feet wide open.

"I'm going to the ATM. I'll be right back."

He slams the front door hard. I fall on the white tile bathroom and bury my legs beneath my knees.

When he comes back, he throws money at me. This is all I have."

Five dollars. It will cost ten. I say nothing. I just want him to go.

Silence.

He pulls up his suit pants, grabs a tie.

"Listen, just lock this up before you go, okay?"

"Esme? Do you hear me?"

I won't acknowledge him. He slams the door.

I stand up and run to the refrigerator. I start searching for something to destroy this place with. I see ketchup in a tall plastic bottle. My first thought is to squirt this ketchup, every ounce, over everything in the house—especially his suit and golf clubs and stock certificates. I want to ruin everything. Then, I decide I can't do that. It is Brett's place, and he has actually been very nice to me. Then, as I'm contemplating the destruction, I see ten dollars across the room under a notebook. Thank God. I grab it. But I can't just take it—I write Brett a note and take out a check from my purse.

"Brett, thank you for letting me stay here. It was very nice to meet you. I took ten dollars. I'm sorry. I had to get a cab. And your asshole friend wouldn't give me five bucks. Here is a check for ten dollars. Thank you, Esme."

I tie my hair back wet, put on eyeliner quickly, mascara, lipstick, pull on a periwinkle dress, slip on black patent leather heels. As fast as I can. I am crying, but no longer sad. I am in a rage, an uncaged animal. I have come unglued.

As I grab my luggage, and place the brass knob of the front door in my palm, I stop. I look at the charcoal black Armani suit to the left, pink Talbot's tie, hanging over the Titleist golf bag. I know what I am going to do now. I have a clarity and economy to my thinking now.

Grab the suit, still on the wood hanger, and I leave, down the winding staircase, out the back door. I walk up to the tall metal blue dumpster and dump it. All of it.

Then, I calmly walk to the corner and hail a cab.

They say the best revenge is living well. No. The best revenge is revenge. He took something from me last night—and now I will take something from him.

I feel better. Already. There is an upside to losing your mind.

When I get back to Washington, I'm clearly disheveled and my eyes are red. I walk to my desk calmly at 10:00. Abbe looks up from her desk and leans toward me.

"You stayed with that asshole, didn't you?"

I hold my hand up. I won't talk about it. He has drained me of all my blood and oxygen and mental acumen. I light a cigarette. Check my voicemail.

One is from Brett. Telling me he is so sorry about Alex and the ten dollars. Of course he won't cash my check. But he'd like to see me again. Would I go out with him in New York sometime? I rub my head. As if. What the fuck? Do these guys think I'm some football they can just pass back and forth? Hit delete.

Next one is from Alex. I sit up erect. He knows. Already? He says that he had to leave work because he forgot something, and he noticed his suit was gone— just gone. What the fuck, Esme? What did you do with it? Call me. I can't fucking believe you.

I don't.

I don't call either one of them back.

In fact, I will never speak to Alex again.

And, the last I heard he went to jail for insider trading.

I'm over hot Alex.

In fact, I'm over hot, period.

Paul

He, who I have seen many times before, walks down the long hallway wearing loose khakis, black Doc Martin boots and a baggy black leather coat. Long black bangs hanging over his left eye. His name was Paul. And Paul will become my all.

As I enter the door of my Constitutional Law class directly across from him, I can't stop staring at him. I mean it's not like I haven't noticed him before, but today is different.

I can't explain why or how, but I just know we are going to be together.

I am in my third year of law school at a competitive and prestigious East Coast university and suffering greatly. Everyone here is so smart. I'm no longer the smartest girl in the room—not by a long shot. The reading is rigorous and the mounting homework is there every single night. There is only one exam at the end of the semester, which we all fear. And my social life isn't so great either. I mean I have few friends, but the demands of law school leave little time for drinking or the movies. It's been a while now, but I still desperately miss college.

I did, until a wealthy friend who grew up here introduced me to an equally wealthy guy who was as handsome as he was rich. He was in commercial real estate and owned a beautiful warehouse condo with lots of open rooms. He was tan with cropped strawberry hair and wore untucked tailored button down shirts coupled with a Rolex watch. He took me to fancy dinners and trendy bars, and I guess you could say for a while at least I had a boyfriend. But despite everything he *had*, I just didn't quite feel it. That familiar feeling I'm had with my college boyfriend snuck up on me—something was just missing. So recently, I ended it. I mean it really just kind of faded out, but I was alone again here on the loneliest planet on the world.

I decided to keep myself busy, to strive to be the best in the class and throw myself into my schoolwork. I participated in class hoping for extra credit, highlighted and outlined my chapters and reminded myself that it would be over by the next year and the pain associated with law school was ephemeral. If I worked hard now, I'd land a great big firm job, make tons of money, and be really happy one day.

Paul was a progressive male and unlike most of the men I met. I first met him (briefly) in my Gender and the Constitution class. He was genuinely interested in women's rights and yearned for a deeper understanding of the rights emanating from the Constitution.

He seemed pensive and thoughtful and always asked questions that I had never even thought about.

One day after class, I was walking out with my friend Jamie who I guess knew him pretty well. She introduced us briefly, and he smiled at me with a half smile, but he didn't seem to want to chat with us much. I found him kind of aloof and anyway, I heard he had a girlfriend who was a graphic artist in town.

A couple of months later, I found out I made the Law Review and was ecstatic. This was paramount—more important even than good grades. It was key to getting a job in a big law firm. It had long been a goal of mine. I knew I was a good writer, but then so was everyone else. I was very shocked (and relieved) when I made it.

Paul made it too. There were only ten of us, and I was told to start coming to the office every day to write and edit prominent professor's articles.

The first day I walked in, I looked around the room for a desk where I would be able to write. As I searched, my eyes met Paul's. He was already sitting in a desk with a red pen, hand editing. I should have known he would already be working.

"Hey," he looked up at me casually and kind of smiled.

"Hey," I responded.

"How are you doing? How was your Christmas break?"

"Good. Mellow. Didn't do a whole lot. How about you?"

"It was okay. Nothing too eventful. Well... I broke up with my girlfriend, but that's about it," He laughed. He didn't even seem to care.

"Oh." I paused wondering why he was telling me this and in such a cavalier manner.

"Well, I'm sorry to hear that."

"Ah, it's okay. It was a long time coming."

"How is the writing coming?" I tried to change the subject.

"It's coming," he laughed.

"What are you writing about?"

"Minimum federal sentencing guidelines and the incarceration of women."

That sounded interesting and exciting to me. I just knew he was liberal and would write about something unique and important.

"That sounds interesting."

"And you?" He put his red pen down.

"Oh just an antitrust issue." I knew I sounded boring. I had worked mostly on health care and technology issues on the Hill and decided that this may be a topic I could write on easily.

"Did you study Economics?" He questioned.

"Ah, no. I mean a little bit of Econ in undergrad, but I worked on some antitrust issues when I was on the Hill so I figured..."

"Yes, I heard you worked on the Hill," he interrupted. "That's really cool."

"Oh thanks. I mean it's not as glamorous as it sounds."

"Well, I think it sounds pretty cool."

"Thanks." I couldn't think of anything else to say.

"Hey, you want to grab a beer sometime?" He suddenly asked.

I couldn't believe it. Did he just ask me out? Was this a date?"

"Sure."

"Great. How about meeting up at Bailey's tomorrow? Five-fifteen? I have Crim law till five."

Bailey's was a local hang out for law students. We would go there after class and have cheap beers and grilled cheese sandwiches. I was still dieting, so I didn't really eat the food. But I did count all the calories in the beer I was consuming so I limited my food intake to things like pretzels, rice cakes and frozen vegetables.

"Great. That works."

"Okay, he stood up putting his backpack on his left shoulder. "I got to split. Have class."

"Okay."

"See you then, Esme."

"See you then."

That night, still in disbelief and confused, I called Jamie. I mean she did know him, and maybe she could provide some insight.

"Oh yeah, I think it's a date." She stated.

"Why do you say that? I mean he may just want to grab a beer."

"Because he thinks you're cute... he told me."

"When?"

"I don't know. A month ago?"

"Well... I thought he had a girlfriend all this time."

"He did... but she was a real nut job artist. I heard he cheated on her actually, and that set her over the edge."

"Really?"

This should have been a red flag, but it wasn't. All I could think about is how non-artsy I was and compared to her, I was really boring.

"Yeah, but just go. Have fun. You never know."

"Okay." I hung up anxious ... excited... thinking about what I would wear the next day.

* * *

During class the next day, I could do nothing but stare at the clock anxiously waiting for 5:00 to arrive. I was getting so excited to see him and wanted to get to know him better. He seemed very mysterious to me, and I started to think about all the questions I would ask him. I decided to wear a short black velvet mini skirt with black tights, high black suede boots and a faded blue jean jacket. I wanted to look casual but also a little sexy and not so boring. I felt a little self-conscious about my legs, but I had finally managed to get into a size four so I was feeling a little better about things.

I decided to arrive at 5:25. I didn't want to beat him there and wait at the bar.

As I entered, he waved sitting in a wooden table at the back of the bar. I walked over slowly trying hard to mask my anxiety.

He looked gorgeous. Better than I had ever seen him. He had cleaned up. Freshly shaven, hair hanging just a little bit—wearing a crisp white oxford shirt over midnight blue jeans. He always looked a bit edgy and gritty to me, but today he looked perfect. I immediately felt unpolished, and my hair was getting frizzy from drops of rain.

"Hey you," He took a sip from his green bottle of beer "I took the liberty of ordering you a beer…" He slid it over to me across the table.

"I hope you like Heineken."

"Yes, I love Heineken." And I did. I wasn't lying this time as I frequently did in the company of men.

"You look very pretty, Esme."

"Oh thank you... you look nice too."

"So, how is your paper coming along?"

"Slowly! Ugh. I hate writing!"

"You hate writing? Yet you wrote for Law Review?"

"Yes. Well… it's important, you know…a"

"Important?" He leaned back in his chair looking at me intently.

"Yes. I mean to get a job, you know…"

"Hmmm. So that's why you applied..."

"Well, I don't *hate* writing, but you do need it for you resume."

"Really?"

He didn't seem to get it. I mean how could he not know this?"

"Yes. I mean… why did you do it?"

"To write. To make a difference. To write about something that would make people take notice."

Immediately, my heart sank. I felt shallow and materialistic. My true nature was coming out now. I wasn't writing for pleasure or to make a difference, I was writing to please some partner in a big law firm.

"Well, that's important too, of course."

"And your antitrust article… What do you want to say?"

"Well… I guess I want to draw attention to the unprecedented pace of mergers in the technology industry and for regulators to take notice of the dangers of that."

"Why?"

"Because… because we need to have competition in the marketplace... so consumers get a fair price."

"Excellent." He said in a professorial tone. "That *is* important."

"And you are writing about the incarceration of women?"

"Yes... and the need to remove mandatory minimum sentencing guidelines. We have too many women and men incarcerated today because of low-level drug crimes. We need to abolish those and give judges flexibility. But the fucking Republicans in Congress won't take up the issue."

"Two more!" He motioned to the waitress.

"I agree with you. That was definitely an issue when I worked in Congress."

I liked that he too hated the Republicans. I was very much hoping this was the case.

"Do you want something to eat? A grilled cheese maybe? I'm going to order something." He picked up the menu.

"Sure. A grilled cheese sounds great."

I couldn't believe I was saying this, but tonight I was actually hungry and wanted to follow suit.

"Great. Let's do it."

We went on to order two more beers and then two more and then two more. I honestly lost count, but I could see that Paul shared the same penchant for alcohol that I did. I was hoping this too was the case. I needed booze to sleep and to sleep with anyone. I had never been comfortable in my own skin, and the alcohol eased my anxieties and helped me with all my reservations.

We went on to discuss the death penalty, the current state of Iraq, and backpacking through Europe. I couldn't get enough of the conversation, and as the booze flowed through my veins, I became more and more talkative and less concerned with what I said.

"You know..." He leaned toward me closer. "I've kind of had a crush on you."

"What?" I laughed leaning closer to him.

"You're very cute." He grabbed my hand.

"I thought you had a girlfriend"

"Did. It's over now. Plus I heard you had a boyfriend."

"I was dating someone, but that was a while ago."

"What happened?"

"Oh I don't know. Nothing *really.* It just wasn't meant to be I think."

"And you?"

"Oh, she was crazy. You know… very jealous. Very volatile. I just couldn't deal anymore"

I pictured him with a Zelda Fitzgerald. She was beautiful and creative and passionate. She was his muse. I was the opposite of this—a materialistic sorority girl who carried a Gucci book bag and wore Laura Ashley dresses. I couldn't imagine us being more different, and I started to feel inadequate.

"I see."

"Let's not talk about her anymore. It's over." He took a big swig of his beer.

"Okay." I wanted to know a lot more, but I didn't want to press the issue.

"Hey, let's get out of here." He abruptly stated and grabbed my hand.

"Okay." I acquiesced.

"Do you want to come over for a drink?"

"Sure."

I needed another drink like I needed a hole in my heart.

Paul lived close to Bailey's so we walked to his house. As we entered the front door, I noticed instantly how messy everything was. There were lots of stacks of white papers on the hardwood floors, stacks of *The New York Times* on the coffee table and a small waste paper basket overflowing with trash.

"Pardon the mess." He kicked some papers over to the side.

"No worries. My apartment is a mess too."

That wasn't exactly a lie. I hated making my bed and rarely dusted. So I actually felt comfortable in my surroundings here.

"Do like Vodka?" He started walking into the tiny kitchen.

"Yes, I do."

Now we were moving on to the hard stuff. Good Lord.

Paul returned with two short Vodka sodas on the rocks.

"Here you go." He grabbed my arm and pulled me down onto the couch.

"Hi." He smiled as he pulled me in closer.

"Hi." I took a big sip of my Vodka. I knew I needed this to relax.

He took my Vodka and set it down on the stained coffee table and started to kiss me.

I felt my body melting and the alcohol rushing to my head.

He started to rub my knee and my then my thigh and put his tongue inside of my mouth.

"Come on. Let's go to my room."

He stood up pulling my arm toward him.

As he pulled me down onto the bed, I knew what was going to happen, and I didn't try to stop it. I was already crazy about him and just succumbed.

"I want to do unspeakable things to your body."

He whispered in my ear as he placed his fingers between my legs.

I reached for him and began to stroke him up and down. I couldn't believe how big he was. I wondered if this was even going to work. But... of course... it did.

He pulled me on top of him. I sat erect, then arched backwards as he pushed deep inside me as he caressed my breasts, then pulled me into him sucking my nipples firmly. He flipped me over on my stomach and pressed himself inside of me. The trusted alcohol was working and in that moment I was not thinking of the cellulite on my ass. I just surrendered to him. After we finished, he pulled me over on top of his chest and stroked my hair.

"That was pretty nice, girl.... Do you want a cigarette?"

"Yes." I sighed.

I love a cigarette after sex and like me, he likes to smoke. Another thing I was hoping for.

We laid in bed smoking and laughing. I could feel the alcohol start to wear off, and I started to fade into sleep. I didn't need the sleeping pills or Xanax that night. I was completely relaxed and content. I had everything I could possibly need.

* * *

Paul and I became inseparable from that night forward. We write together in the afternoons in the living room of my apartment. I sit on the futon couch, and he sits in the big oversized chair until we can't resist each other anymore. We proof each other's work, and Paul is a diligent editor. Sometimes I feel like shit when I look at all the red marks, but I know he is right. He is making me a better writer.

At night, I cook him dinner, and we have sex again after drinking red wine and watching foreign films. Paul buys me Elvis Costello and Miles Davis CDs and teaches me a lot about music. He seems to know so much about so many things.

I start to dissolve into him and lose myself as well as my friends.

"You never want to work out with me anymore. What's up?" My closest friend Renee asks me one day after class.

Renee has been a godsend… introducing me to so many people and breaking me out of my shell. It's all because of her that I even have any friends. We used to have a ritual of skipping out of our Securities Regulation class and going to the gym, doing the Stairmaster for 45 or 50 minutes and then lifting weights. We always rewarded ourselves with Chinese food and red wine afterwards. But lately, I'm not really working out at all, and I haven't seen Renee in two weeks.

"I'm really sorry. I've just been busy, and I haven't been exercising. Law Review… all this work."

"That's bullshit, and you know it. You're always with Paul."

"That's not true. I am usually at the Law Review office editing articles."

"I don't buy it. He's such a poser. I wish you would just lose him."

"Renee… he's not."

Renee has always felt that Paul pretends to be something he's not. She thinks he's pretentious and arrogant and thinks he's better than everyone else. But he's just shy and somewhat aloof. Sometimes he comes off the wrong way to people, but there's so much good in him. I wish she could just see it.

"And he has no friends. He wants *you* to have no friends too."

Paul doesn't have any friends really. I mean he used to hang out with his roommate some, but now he's practically living with me, and when I'm not with him, he leaves voicemails on my answering machine looking for me. I feel guilty when I leave him, and I've become that girl I said I never would be—the one that ditches her friends for a guy. But it's not such a sacrifice. I do want to be with him all the time. We're in love now, and no one understands it.

At night, when Paul showers, I lie in my bed on top of my blue Laura Ashley comforter and thank God that I have met my soul mate. I feel like I am the luckiest girl in the world.

Time flies by. Third year is almost over, and I am still with Paul. However, as fall creeps into spring, and the seasons change, so does Paul.

We go out one night together to Bailey's to meet a bunch of classmates for drinks. We enter the bar holding hands. Everyone knows we are a couple. We have never tried to hide it. In fact, I want *everyone* to know it.

Paul leaves me for a while to talk to his friend who is a lesbian and frequently teases him that she wants his baby one day. I sit at the bar and hang out with my friend Matthew who is also on Law Review with us. He used to be in my study group until I dropped out and started studying with Paul.

"Let me get you a drink, Esme." He leans into the bar and waves at the bartender.

"You don't have to get me a drink!" I protest.

I am feeling tipsy. Paul and I already had a bottle of Chardonnay at home.

"I want to." He puts his hand on top of my head and messes up my hair.

"What would you like?"

"Oh, I guess a Vodka soda."

As usual, I start to go right for the hard stuff. Matthew comes from a wealthy East Coast family and unlike me, he's not here on student loans. He always has the best of everything and orders me a Grey Goose martini.

"A martini?" I laugh.

"Yes, I think you need a stiff drink." He touches my arm playfully.

I look across the bar for Paul and see him looking directly at me. I smile his way, but he just keeps staring at me.

"So how's life, Esme Oliver?" He hands me my martini.

"Thank you. All is good. What about you?"

"I don't know... I'd be better if I saw you more often. I miss you in study group. I miss your outlines!"

"Aw, that's really sweet. I've just been so busy with Law Review. I haven't even been outlining this semester!"

"So... how are things with Paul?"

"Good. I mean great."

"Good to hear."

He doesn't seem convinced. Suddenly I feel a hand on top of my shoulder.

"Hey," It's Paul. "Hey Matt."

"Hey Paul. What's going on?"

"Nothing much. But listen, we have to go now."

Paul takes my martini and puts it down on the counter firmly. It spills.

"I haven't finished my drink." I am annoyed. I don't want to go.

"Come on, Esme. I'm tired. I want to get out of here."

I get up to go and thank Matthew for the drink that I covet and will never have.

I grab my purse and my cardigan and walk down the brick stair entrance with Paul.

He is in rage.

"What the *fuck* Esme?" He stops in the middle of the street.

"What do you mean 'what the *fuck*?'"

"You are sitting there…. Just sitting there at the bar flirting… flirting with Matthew…. Right in front of my fucking face."

"What are you talking about? We are just friends."

"That's bullshit. He's hot for you. And you know it. And you… you are a *huge* flirt."

"I didn't do anything, Paul. Jesus."

"Yes, you did. I saw him touching you. I saw the way you were looking at him."

"I wasn't looking at him in any way. I don't know what you are talking about."

"Just shut up, Esme. You know what you did."

"No you, shut up. I did nothing. You're being totally insane."

"You know what? I'm not coming over tonight… just go home."

69

"Fine Paul. That's fine."

I walk home and crawl into bed alone and begin to sob on my pillow. I can't understand why Paul has done this to me… why he's suddenly becoming so possessive and so suspicious.

But I miss him. I'm so used to him lying here next to me with his long arm draped over my waist. I fear I'm losing him and that he's going to break up with me tomorrow. I can't imagine my life without him.

The next day I check my messages over and over again. Nothing from Paul. My heart sinks deeper and deeper. I reach for the Vodka and lay in my bed listening the CDs he has bought me that we had played together.

Finally, he calls. He tells me he wants to meet up and talk. I don't think this sounds good, and I grow increasingly paranoid that he is going to break up with me, but I agree.

Ironically, he asks me to meet him at Bailey's where this whole mess started. I have to sober up fast. I haven't eaten a thing all day and have been hitting the bottle hard. I shower rapidly and rub concealer on the purple hollows under my eyes.

I make some coffee and try to sober up.

When I arrive, he is waiting for me at the bar. He has already ordered us both a Heineken. I know I shouldn't be drinking anymore today, but I take the bottle immediately and start drinking the beer. I need to be in an altered state fast to deal with this.

"Listen," He starts. "I'm sorry about how things went down. I was just really pissed off when I saw you two at the bar."

I listen and sip my beer again.

"I just don't trust you sometimes... when you are around other guys."

"Why don't you trust me?"

"I don't know. I just worry you're going to meet someone else and leave me."

"Who would I meet? What are you talking about? Can't you see that I don't want to be with anyone except you?"

I reach for his arm trying to reassure him.

"I don't know what's wrong with me." He rubs he hands through his long bangs. "I just don't want to lose you... ever."

"You're not going to lose me, Paul. I'm crazy about you. You must know that."

"You're so beautiful." He kisses my hand. "What was I thinking?"

And with that we go back to my apartment and drink more and have sex and pass out. Everything is perfect again. I don't think to push back. I don't think to question him for being such a psychopath. I am just so relieved he's back here with me again.

* * *

It's near the end of our third and final year, and there are all those things that come with end of the year and graduation—awards, banquets, and ceremonies. The Law Review announces it too will be having a banquet. An award will be given to the best writer, and this immediately seems to interest Paul way more than it does me. We have both been published twice now, and most of our classmates haven't even been published once. But I could care less about what the Law Review thinks of me really, and I don't care about their dumb awards.

"Who cares?" I tell Paul on our way home from class. "Like I care what they think of my writing! I don't even want to go to the damn thing."

And I don't. I am happy in my bubble with Paul. I would rather stay in and drink wine and watch independent films, but Paul really wants to go. He thinks it's important for us to show up.

So I slip on my long black dress with a slit up the left side and strappy black heels. I put my hair into a loose bun and put on my favorite strand of pearls. I try to look elegant and sexy for Paul. He tells me how beautiful I look and pulls my hand into his as we enter the banquet hall.

Paul and I are lucky. We are seated a table with fun people, and we start to drink a lot of red wine. As usual, I pick at my food not really wanting to eat. And the more I drink, the happier I feel, and my disdain for the event starts to wane. Paul seems to be enjoying it; he's talking to people a lot more than usual. But the all of the speeches and awards are boring me. I get up to go outside and have a cigarette.

"Where are you going?" Paul grabs my arm.

"I'm going outside to have a cigarette."

"Okay." He lets go of my arm.

"Come with me. I need some air."

"Okay. Okay." He stands up.

It seems like Paul and I are always outside smoking these days and probably at not the most appropriate of times. But the banquet is making me claustrophobic, and I just need to escape. I just shouldn't have taken Paul with me.

Paul lights a cigarette for me and hands it to me. I start to smoke and roll my eyes and tell him how sick I am of being there. He tells me it won't be much longer. There are just a few more awards left—best writer being one of them. We stay outside for a while—too long actually. When we walk back into the atrium, I see that our chief editor has already announced the best writer award, and of course, it was Paul. I feel my heart sink and start to panic. This is the award—the one I know he really wanted. And now because of me, we have missed the presentation.

I immediately dash off and grab our chief's editor's arm.

"Listen, you have to announce this again.... Paul was outside. He missed the award."

"I'm not sure we can do this again. I mean we already announced it."

"You have to," I plead. "You have to let him get his award!"

I know Paul will want the acknowledgement and the praise of his classmates. I'm determined to see this happen.

"Okay, let me announce it one more time..."

Paul walks to the podium and takes the certificate. He does not look proud or happy. He looks angry, and I can't understand why. I thought this was what he wanted.

"Congratulations!" I stand up and smile as he makes his way back to our table, but he just stares at me and says nothing.

"What's wrong?" I touch his shoulder.

"Why in the fuck did you say something? Why did you embarrass me?" He whispers in my ear.

"I don't know what you're talking about!"

"I don't know why you did that... why you had to embarrass me in front of all these people."

"I just wanted you to get your award! It was my fault we were outside to begin with."

"I just want to go." He stands up and grabs his jacket.

"Let's go," He grabs my hand.

We start to walk home in the slowly drizzling rain, and Paul lights a cigarette and starts screaming at me.

"I mean, what the fuck, Esme? You are the one who said these awards are stupid. You are the one who made fun of the whole thing."

"They are stupid to me. But I know they mean something to you. I'm proud of you. I knew you would win."

"No... you are jealous. That's why you did this.... Because you think you should have won."

"Are you fucking kidding me?"

"No, I'm not. This is why you embarrassed me in front of all those people."

"I wanted you to get credit! Jesus Christ, Paul, what is wrong with you?"

"I don't believe you." He starts to walk faster and faster in front of me. "I'm going home tonight. Don't follow me."

My heart drops. It's that same feeling again. I have no idea what I have done wrong, but I just know that this time he's going to leave me for good. I don't fight it. I walk home alone and again just wait for him to call.

* * *

The next day Paul calls just like he did before. I tell him over and over again how proud I am of him, and I try to convince him that I never ever wanted the award, but I can tell he still doesn't believe me. He never really apologizes for the things he said. I can tell he feels no remorse or regret. I think about it over and over again, and I realize that maybe I could have handled it differently. Maybe I should not have drawn attention to the situation and have just let it go. I blame myself and beg him to come back home.

Things go back to usual pretty rapidly. Paul and I spend our nights cramming for finals and our days sleeping in. We are graduating and soon will begin our bar review classes. I have, as I planned so carefully, landed a job with a big law firm in Boston, and they are paying for my Bar review classes as well as my move after the summer ends. Paul, however, despite his better grades and his published works, did not land a law firm job. He didn't get past his initial interviews with any of them. He ran out of options and finally accepted a clerkship with a judge in Providence. Soon we will be living in separate cities, and soon I will be making twice as much as Paul.

I feel awful about how things turned out. I'm nervous about everything especially being in separate cities next year.

So I decide to maximize my summer with Paul. I decide to quit attending the Bar review classes as soon as they start and convince Paul to do the same. The classes are long and tedious and eating up most of our day.

"We can just read this stuff or listen to the tapes later." I tell Paul.

"I'm so burnt out of school, Paul. I just want to chill."

I should be afraid though. My new firm is paying for these classes and expecting me to pass the bar and be willing and able to work my ass off come September. But I'm not nervous. I blow off the Bar review classes just like I blew off many classes over this past year to hang out with Paul. I know I have a good memory and am good at cramming. I tell myself I can pull it all together at the end. I tell him we'll start studying right after the fourth of July. We have three weeks then, and that's plenty of time. Plus we're always tired and hung over in the morning, and it's just impossible to be at class at 8:30 a.m.

We're running out of money though as my student loans are drying up. I sign up for a Bar review loan so I can buy groceries and wine and cook for Paul every night.

Paul finally acquiesces to my plan, and we start our summer together alone free from the encumbrances of school or work. We have both been dying to read anything besides the law so we lay in my bed during the day reading books—I get Mary Karr's *The Liars' Club*, and Paul starts the daunting task of reading David Foster Wallace's *Infinite Jest*. I stay in my nightgown most of the day reading and drinking white wine and having sex with Paul. Some days we get up and smoke pot and go on long bike rides in the rolling hills of our campus. At night, I make hummus and tabouli from scratch and marinate chicken breasts. I try to make sure I cook all his favorites. Paul never helps me do anything really, but I don't mind. We are all alone now. We don't see our friends anymore. They are all busy studying for the bar.

I like it this way though. I don't need anything more than Paul.

"What are we going to do when the summer ends?" I turn to over to Paul one afternoon throwing my book on the hardwood floor.

"I'm so sad."

"It will be fine." He rubs the hair back that is falling in my eyes. "We'll figure it out, babe."

"But how? You're going to be in Providence."

"I'll come visit you every weekend."

"Do you promise?" I roll over and grab his hand tightly.

"Yes, of course. We're going to be together. Don't worry."

I feel relieved. Paul wants to be with me forever. We will be apart but not for long. His clerkship is only one year, and then he can move to Boston, and we can get married and buy a Brownstone in the city.

* * *

The first year out of law school turns out to be brutal. After all this work, my dream job and dream life are not materializing—in fact, quite the opposite. For the first three months of my job, I am completely ignored by all the partners. No one seems to have *any* work to give me, and a senior partner there is waiting to put me on a bit health care deal that is emerging soon. So I just sit there at work stressing out about the billable hours I'm not accruing and missing Paul and our afternoon bike rides.

Paul, on the other hand, is thriving at work although he's making no money, which he reminds me of constantly. I guess his co-clerk isn't that bright or driven so he's taking all the good cases and writing brilliant opinions that the judge just signs off.

I buy a brick Brownstone with high ceilings and exposed brick walls in a new neighborhood walking distance from work, and on the weekends Paul comes to visit me. We have a great life on the weekends. It's just like it was in law school. We walk to trendy restaurants, watch Indie films and have sex twice a day. I buy him lots of nice clothes for work because I know he can't afford them. We start to look at houses in nearby suburbs and talk about what it will be like when we get married and both have law firm jobs. I am determined to help him get a job like mine, and then we can afford a really nice house and start a family. I have *everything* mapped out.

Eventually, the merger heats up, and I get sent to Mass General to work on its acquisition of physician practices. I review documents for hours looking for onerous provisions in contracts and am bored to tears. I can't believe this is what I signed up for when I joined the corporate law group. I thought I'd be doing challenging antitrust cases and arguing before federal courts. Instead, I am stuck alone all day in a hospital basement with nothing to keep me company but a big stack of papers. At lunch, however, I am permitted to go upstairs and eat, with the other lawyers, in the doctor's dining room. The food is way better than the cafeteria, and I get to meet a lot of doctors working on riveting things and new discoveries.

I am one of youngest and one of the only females

there, so I get a lot of looks every time I walk in the door. I don't really pay attention to the attention though. All I can think of is Paul.

Paul is becoming increasingly irritated with his co-clerk, Liz, and complains about her every single night.

"I wish she could be more like you, and then this job would be so much easier." He sighs on the phone.

"She's just not motivated... at all. So I just take all the good cases."

"Well... at least you are getting the good stuff."

I try to look on the bright side. I'm still jealous that at least he likes his job.

"I just can't stand working with her, Esme. And every time somebody brings doughnuts into the office, she's dashes for them."

"Well, I hate my job, period. It's awful being at that hospital every day, and now I think they are going to assign me to the partner who is there all day, so that means I will be there till who knows when."

"I don't like you working there."

"Why not?"

"Because I feel like you're going to meet someone there... a doctor."

"Paul, geez. I barely see anyone there. I'm always reviewing documents."

"I know you go to that doctor's dining room, Esme. I bet those doctors flirt with you too."

"No, they don't. I barely speak to them, Paul. You're being crazy."

And he is. I don't know why I don't see it, or maybe I do and just don't care. But he's always paranoid that I'm going to meet someone else. I have no idea where this comes from because I'm so incredibly loyal, but it comes up every so often and drives me nuts.

"I have to go. I have some more research to do..."

He seems to want off the phone suddenly, and I really don't want to hang up yet, but I also don't want to fight, and I can feel a fight coming on.

"Okay. Love you. Miss you."

"Love you too, babe."

As the year progresses, I am getting more and more anxious about Paul finding a job here. His clerkship will end in June, and if he is to move here in the fall, he has to start interviewing now, yet he's doing nothing about it. As usual, I take over and start reaching out to the firms that I interviewed with last year on campus and to see if they will meet with Paul. I mean there's no reason he can't get a job here—he has slightly better grades than me and he did publish twice on Law Review. I still have no idea why his interviews last year didn't result in a job like mine did. But I'm determined to find him a job.

"Listen," I call him. "I reached out to the partner I interviewed with a McElvey & Brown last year. I sent him your resume, and he wants to meet with you."

I really pulled some strings to make this happen and thought Paul would be thrilled.

"Uhm... I don't know, Esme. I'm not really that interested in McElvey."

"Why? It's a great firm. They have a great litigation department. I think you'd be a great litigator."

"You do, huh?"

"Yes, I do."

"Why is that?"

"Because you are great writer! You can write great briefs. Plus, you like to argue." I laugh.

"I don't know. I'll think about it."

I am annoyed. He isn't moving at all on this, and time is running out.

"Do you want me to reach out to Holster Holmes? I know a few people there… "

"No, not really. You know… what I really want is to work at your firm."

"My firm? What?"

"Yes. I would like that. I didn't get an interview on campus though."

"Paul, I don't think it's a good idea for us to work at the same law firm."

"Why? Why would you say that? There are plenty of married partners at your firm."

"Well... I don't know. It would just be awkward. I think McElvey would be a better fit for you."

"I don't think you know what a good fit for me is."

"What is that supposed to mean?"

"You are always trying to tell me what to do... what will be best for me."

"Paul... I'm just trying to get you a job here... so we can be together."

"Let me think about it."

The next day I start to panic. Why does he want to come to *my* firm? I already told him it's not that great here. But for me, it's imperative I stay for a while. They have the best reputation in health care in all of Boston. What is something happens? What if we broke up or got divorced? We would be stuck together. Why can't he just look somewhere else?

But Paul continues to push it with me. He wants to come to my firm. He wants me to help him. So I do.

I realize that first I have to figure out what department he will be in so I can approach the department chair. *I* decide on Litigation. I told Paul he'd be great at that, but I don't really know that to be the case. It seems all he wants to do is write liberal opinions and focus more on Constitutional law, which we don't even have here.

I approach Jeffrey Jackson, the arrogant and eccentric head of Litigation. He has always seemed to like me. I feel like he'll do me this one favor and interview Paul.

"Send me his resume, Esme." I'll look it over. He tells me when I stop by his office.

"Okay. I will. Thank you!"

"So … are you serious with this guy?"

"Yes. Yes, we are serious."

"Going to marry him?"

"Yes... eventually."

"Okay then. Let me look it over. I'll get back to you."

I tell Paul that I got his resume to Jeffrey, and he is thrilled. For once, he doesn't seem ambivalent about his career or annoyed with me. I'm still very nervous about this, but I want to make him happy.

One week later, Jeffrey stops by my office and tells me he will interview Paul.

"Impressive resume, Esme. But tell me this, why didn't he get an interview on campus last year?"

"I don't know.... I have no idea. I mean he did get interviews with the other big firms."

"Did he get an offer?"

"No." I sigh. I know this isn't a good sign.

"Okay. Well…. because it's you. I'll bring him in."

"Thank you so much Jeffrey!"

Paul ends up getting the interview and then shortly thereafter the job. My heart sinks when he gets the offer. Paul didn't even know that he wanted to be a litigator. But I know I made this all happen for him despite my reservations. I still can't help thinking how bad things would be if we ever got divorced and had to work together. But then I am always waiting for the floor to drop beneath me. Nothing bad is going to happen. Plus there are plenty of married couples here. It will be fine.

Paul is ecstatic. He sends me a dozen red roses and tells me how much he loves me. He can't wait to start and talks about it all the time. I hate hearing about it. I am still in the basement and have rapidly learned that money doesn't make you happy. I'm miserable at work but happy that at least Paul is moving here so we can finally be together again.

Almost every night on the phone Paul complains to me about Liz. He tells me she's lazy and leaves every night right at five. He laments the workload and how he's responsible for so much of it now.

"At least I'll be out of here soon with all this bullshit. I honestly can't wait to start."

I warn him about the hours and the grunt work at the firm, but he just gets agitated and tells me I'm being negative. I try to say very little. Instead I start looking at places for us to live and send Paul photos and more photos of houses.

As the days pass, I become increasingly depressed. The work I'm doing on a daily basis is so unfulfilling.

I'm learning nothing and fear my mind is atrophying. I don't have much time for lunch so I sneak out to the McDonald's on campus and get small fries, which I dip in ketchup and never finish. I try to run after work, but often, I'm just so tired that I just lay on my sofa drinking red wine. And it seems that Paul is always so busy at work now. He doesn't call me every single night anymore, and I just feel this growing distance between us, which is making me even more depressed.

It's the day of our anniversary, and I am so excited. I have sent Paul bundles of clothes—corduroy pants, Thomas Pink ties and J.Crew sweaters. I know he still needs clothes for work, and I am making so much more money than he is so I'm happy to do it. I go to the dungeon at work and can't wait to get home to see what he has done for me. I expect flowers or perfume or something thoughtful that I haven't even thought of. But when I get home and check my mail, there is nothing—no card, no gift. I rush to my front door looking for flowers or some sort of package, but there is nothing. How could he forget? How could he blow off our anniversary?

As I enter my home, the phone rings. It is Paul.

"Esme… Esme… I got your gift. I'm such an asshole … such an asshole."

"You forgot."

"I've just been so slammed at work. I don't even know what day it is anymore. I'm so sorry. I love the clothes you sent. You are so sweet."

"I can't believe you forgot our anniversary. I just cannot fucking believe it."

"Babe, let me make it up to you. I'll take you to a nice dinner this weekend."

"Forget it. It's too late."

I hang up the phone and start crying. He's changing. He's pulling away, and I don't know why. I just got him a fucking job, and we're supposed to be making plans to get married and buy a house. Now all he seems to care about is the fucking job.

There will be no "nice dinner" out. Paul cancels that weekend. He says he can't come to Boston because he just has so much work to do before he starts his new job.

"I'm sorry, babe. I have, no lie, like ten cases I have to sift through this weekend. I wouldn't be any fun."

He apologizes, but I don't believe him. He's never worked this hard, and he's always balanced his workload well, which is why I got to see him every weekend. I spend my weekend alone running on the river, smoking cigarettes and drinking red wine. I realize these endeavors are counterproductive, but I don't care. I can do both smoking and running with relative ease. I don't really have that many friends in Boston. I mean some classmates have settled here, but it's not like I have reached out to them. I spend all my free time with Paul.

I become suspicious. I realize I am now turning into him, and this may just all just be in my head, but my gut tells me something is wrong. For some reason, I decide to reach out to Jamie, my law school classmate who I haven't talked to in a long time. We are not really friends, but she too lives in Providence, and I know she has dinner from time to time with Paul. They are friends, and maybe she will know why he's acting so weird. I pick up my phone and call her

Saturday evening. I am short and direct. I just need to know.

"He doesn't even come visit me anymore. He used to come every single weekend."

"Listen Esme... I don't know what is going on with you guys. Maybe he's just working a lot now before he starts his new job."

"That's bullshit. He has always worked hard, and he has always had time for me."

"Listen... this is between you two. I don't want to get into the middle of it."

She knows something—something important. I am determined to get it out of her.

"I know you know something.... Just tell me Jamie."

She pauses.

"I think Paul should be the one to talk to you about this, Esme."

"What is it, Jamie? I need to know."

I feel my heart drop to the floor. I just know this is going to be something awful.

"Well, I saw him the other night at the opera. I was there too."

"At the opera? Paul doesn't go to the opera. Are you sure it was him?"

"Positive."

"What?"

"Esme, he was there. He was with Liz."

"Liz? Liz Cummings... his co-clerk?"

"Yes."

"How could that be? That makes no sense. He can't stand her. Plus she's engaged. We were actually invited to her wedding this summer."

"I don't know. I'm not sure why she wasn't there with her fiancée."

"This just doesn't make sense. I'm sure they went as friends. Maybe she needed a date?"

"They were holding hands, Esme."

I hear the words. I feel myself falling to the ground. I grab the arm of my sofa to hold myself up.

"What? Are you sure? Are you sure you saw *them*?"

"Yes. I'm sure. Esme... I'm so sorry to have to tell you this. You really should talk to Paul."

"Thank you, Jamie. I have to go."

I hang up. I fall to the floor and cover my face. How could this be true? After all the horrible things he has said to me about Liz and now he's holding her hand at the opera? Is he cheating on me? I should have seen this coming. I mean he cheated on his last girlfriend. Why wouldn't he cheat on me?

And now he's coming to my firm. I will have to see him every day. I will have to go to firm retreats with him. What if he decides to stay forever? My worst nightmare has come true.

I want to call Paul. I want to rip him a new asshole. I want all the details. I want him to love me like he used to. But I do nothing. I decide I will wait... until he calls.

Then I will find out everything.

So I wait. On Sunday he doesn't call. He's fucking her right now. He's in love with her. She's pregnant and moving here with him. All things awful go through my mind.

I go back to work on Monday. Things at least are getting better there. I no longer have to go to the hospital and am back at the firm getting some interesting assignments from various partners. I'm finally out of the dungeon and getting to know people at work. But now that I'm back at the firm, I am full of dread as I know soon I will be seeing Paul here. I try to draft a contract, but I can't focus. I keep checking my email to see if Paul has written, and he hasn't. It's all I can to keep myself still and not write an email to him. But I will wait.

That night Paul finally calls. He feigns enthusiasm and asks me all about my day at work. He tells me how he's sorry he checked out all weekend, but he was just working so hard. I listen to the bullshit, and then I snap.

"I don't believe you."

"Believe what? I told you I had ten cases to go through!"

"I don't believe you, Paul. You are lying to me."

"What the fuck, Esme?"

"Why were you at the opera with Liz?"

Dead silence.

"I know you were there with her. By the way, I thought you *hated* her."

"She had an extra ticket, Esme and it was *La Boheme* which I actually really wanted to see."

"So why were you holding her hand?"

"What the fuck, Esme? Where are you getting this information? Are you spying on me now?"

"I know you were holding her hand. Don't lie to me, Paul. Just don't lie to me anymore."

He says nothing. And then I know it's all true.

"Are you seeing her? Are you?"

"We've been hanging out some, yes."

"Behind my back? And this is why you didn't come this weekend! It has nothing to do with your work. I thought you loved me. I thought we were building a future together. Don't you love me anymore?"

"Esme... don't. Don't do this."

"No. I want to know. Do you still love me?"

"Esme, you have changed."

"Changed? I have changed?"

"Yes... you are not the same person I fell in love with."

"How have I changed?"

"It's everything... you have to go to the nicest restaurants. Your family is the same way. You make fun of everyone. You have to carry expensive handbags..."

"What in the hell are you talking to? You're breaking up with me because I have a Gucci handbag?"

"It's just that I used to think you were so sweet... you cooked dinner for me all the time. You took care of me. Now... I don't know... you just seem arrogant."

"I'm arrogant? I'm arrogant? You're the one who *has* to be the best writer... who thinks he is the best writer."

"See? This is what I'm talking about... you are always bashing me. I don't get know why you do this."

"Are you breaking up with me Paul? Are you?"

I feel the tears well up in my eyes. I can't believe he's leaving me after all I have done for him.

"I don't know Esme... I don't know what I want. I need time to think."

"I don't want you coming here. I don't want you coming to my firm. Stay in Providence."

"I'm starting my job there in four months, Esme. I don't know what you expect me to do about that."

"No! No! I don't want you coming. This is my firm. You wouldn't even have this job if it wasn't for me, and I don't want you coming here now. I told you I never wanted you here... and now you do this."

"I was coming to the firm for the work... with or without you."

"That's not true. I told Jeffrey to interview you because we were getting married."

"You may have made the introduction for me, Esme, but I got the job."

"Fuck you, Paul. You used me to get what you wanted. You have always used me... and all you did was tell me how much you hated Liz. You lied to me about that too."

"Listen, I have to go... I need to think. I'll call you later this week."

I slam down the phone.

It's all true. He has cheated on me, and now he's not only leaving me, he's moving here and joining my firm. I light up a cigarette and pour a tall glass of Vodka on the rocks. After everything I have done for him, he now thinks I'm arrogant. I drink and drink until I pass out on the couch in my navy blue suit. I wake up with a roaring headache and a breaking heart—I remember that this wasn't just a bad dream. This is my reality now.

* * *

Days and then weeks pass. I never hear from Paul. He never does call me back. So I guess this is how it ends with us. I do hear stories about him at work. The Litigation partners are anxiously awaiting his arrival. Even though he is in Rhode Island and had plenty of firms there interested in him, he has nevertheless decided to come here.

And it only gets worse. I learn his is bringing her with him. They are looking for apartments now downtown, and she is looking at some smaller firms in Boston. I doubt she will even work. She's so dumb. And anyway, he will be making plenty of money.

It's only a few months now till he arrives with her. I desperately feel like I need a boyfriend before he gets here. I just have to move on and be happy again. I can't be alone when comes.

So I start to date, and often. I meet a resident neurologist at the hospital, and we start spending a lot of time together as he lives right down the street from me.

But he's from family money and rich and self-centered, and we start to fight about the way he talks to the nurses when they page him. I can't stand it. I think about Paul and how he always wanted to protect those who were under him. I could never see him talking to his secretary like this. So I break up with him only to move rapidly to one of my law firm friend's brother. He's a meathead and obsessed with tailgating at football games on the weekends, but I sleep with him anyway and drink a lot of beer. I convince myself that I don't need an intellectual—that it's more important to be with someone who treats you well. And although he's pretty stupid, he is really nice to me.

But somehow I always go back to Paul. I compare everyone to Paul and start to wonder if it is even possible for me to ever fall in love again. I wonder if he has changed his mind—if he will come back to me and dump that piece of white trash.

My body and my mind start to break down as I anticipate his arrival. I am losing a lot of weight without even trying, and the associates at the firm are talking about me. One of my friends there tells me that I look too thin, and people are starting to worry about me. I can't concentrate at work. I think about Paul coming and start to cry. I just know I'm going to get fired. I just wish I could go back to the dungeon at the hospital where no one could see me.

After work, I lie on my hardwood floors and cry and chain smoke cigarettes. I keep waiting for the email or the phone call—for some kind of explanation, but it never arrives. I leaf through the photos of houses we explored and feel sick to my stomach again. My parents now know about the situation, and they call me every day to make sure I'm okay. I'm not, and everyone knows I'm just not getting better. Finally, one evening my dad flies into Boston and shows up at my house. My parents have been divorced for years, and I have always been much closer to my father, a successful entrepreneur who has always taken care of me.

"Esme, you have to stop drinking so much." He says as I pour my second glass of red wine.

"I can tell when we are on the phone that you are drinking."

"So what, Dad? It helps me go to sleep."

"You are self-medicating."

"Maybe I learned it from you." I fire back bringing up his previous drinking problem.

"I quit drinking three years ago…. I just want you to watch it. I'm very concerned about you, honey."

"Dad, I can't take this anymore. I really can't. Paul... he's moving here in like two months. And I'm going to have to see him at the firm every day."

"Esme, Paul is an asshole. He's always been an asshole. You need to be grateful. He did you a big favor."

"He's not an asshole, Dad. You just don't know him."

"Well, look at what he did to you! Who does that? He could have taken a job in Providence... or another firm in Boston!"

"I know. I know that."

"Listen, honey. You are not well. I want you to see someone."

"See who, Dad?"

"A psychiatrist... I found a good one at Mass General, and I think she can help you."

"You want me to see a shrink, Dad?"

"Yes, just to help you get through this bad time. I think it will help."

"So you want to medicate me?"

"I think that's up to the doctor not me. But I do think an antidepressant could help you right now."

"I'm not going to see a shrink. I'll get through it. I will. I promise."

However, a few days later after he has left and I am alone again, I realize that I have to do *something* to feel better. I make the appointment at Mass General with the psychiatrist my father has found. Maybe I do need an antidepressant. Maybe then at least I'll stop crying during the day at work.

When I meet with the psychiatrist, she tell me this:

93

"Paul is a very bad person, Esme. He's very selfish, and he's a narcissist. You are better off without this type of person in your life. Trust me."

"I still love him though."

"And soon, I bet by the time you are 31, you will be engaged and much happier with someone else."

"I doubt it. I don't connect easily with men. Paul was the exception."

And I prove myself to be right. It is Paul who will go on to be very happy... not me.

She gives me Wellbutrin. It's also supposed to help me quit smoking, and I know that's gotten out of control. I take it every day but feel nothing really. Suddenly though, it kicks in. I stop crying at work. I don't crave the cigarettes or booze as much. But it doesn't dull the pain much. I still miss Paul and dread the day I will have to see him again.

* * *

It's September now. The fall is here and soon Paul will be arriving. All my attempts to get a new boyfriend before his arrival have been exercises in futility. There is no one in my life. There isn't even anyone on the horizon. At least Paul and I are on different floors and different departments. Thank God for that. Hopefully, I won't run into him.

I do learn when he joins the firm. There is a lot of buzz at work about the new associates coming in, and I hear Paul's name often. He's written a lot of opinions now, and the Litigation partners seem genuinely excited about his arrival.

I stay in my office most of the time. I pack my

lunch so I don't have to go downstairs to the snack room for fear of running into Paul. I avoid everyone in Litigation because I don't want to hear a word about Paul.

One day I go to the law library to pick up a stack of cases I have printed out. I sit down at a table for a while and skim through a book that might help me with my current case. Then suddenly, I look up and it's Paul. He is holding my cases and hands them to me gently.

"Hi, Esme."

I say nothing.

"How are you? You look great. You changed your hair."

"Leave me alone, Paul. Just leave me alone." I grab my cases and stand up.

"Esme, I hope you are all right. I just wanted to see you."

"I have to go."

And with that the tears start to cascade. I can' t believe he is actually in front of me and that we are not together.

I also know that I can no longer live here.

* * *

I use the same determination I had to make Law Review to get out of this town. It's not the firm I need to leave, it's Boston. I can't be here anymore. I can't bear the thought of running into them at restaurants or Bar events or the movies. Boston isn't that big, and I can't bear the thought of seeing them together out and about on the town. It's bad enough I had to see him at work.

Instead of working on mergers, I work on my resume. I don't really care about my billable hours anyway because I know I'm leaving soon. And thankfully, I'm really good at editing resumes. I've done it for a ton of my friends. And I can write fast so that's another good thing. I start to send out resumes to cities that I might like to live in with good health care markets.

I go to work every day and research cities and firms. I don't feel so depressed anymore because I know I am getting out of here soon. I narrow it down to five cities, but after all these banal hours, I now know I want a city where I can have some semblance of a life. New York City is tempting to me as it always has been, but I just know I will be working harder there than I am in Boston, and that's just too much. I decide I want out of the East coast for a simpler, better life.

In the end, believe it or not, I decide on Nashville. There are a lot of hospitals there and a robust health care market as well as a music scene. I also have one sorority sister from college living there now, and she loves it. And that's a start. As I start to interview there, my father, still concerned with my mental health, calls me.

"Esme, are you sure you really want to leave Boston? Your life is there, your friends, your house… you don't want him to drive you out of the city you love."

"Dad, I have to get out of here. It's time. It's time for me to move on... to start a new life."

"I hear you are moving south. That is so far away from me. Are you sure this is what you want?"

"Yes. I've been looking at Atlanta, Nashville, and Charlotte. They have good weather, Dad, and people there don't work all the time. Plus it's way cheaper than Boston."

"Esme, you are a northern girl. I cannot see you living in the south. It's so backward there."

My father grew up in Boston and is the quintessential New Englander. He retired early and moved to Portland, Maine—summers in Cape Cod and can't imagine a world outside of New England. But I am tired of working this hard for a small house without a yard. I want to try something new. I mean maybe all of this awful stuff could have happened with Paul so I could move somewhere better—somewhere that suits me where I may actually be happier. I'm trying now at least to look at the bright side of all of this.

Meanwhile, Paul is adapting well at the firm and in Boston. They have him working on the most complicated and high profile asbestos litigation case. I hear that Liz is here now too, and they bought a house in the suburbs—the same neighborhood I looked at. I prepare myself. I know she will be pregnant soon. And she will have boys which is what we always talked about.

Finally, I get the letter in the mail. It's from a big law firm in Nashville that I have interviewed with several times. They are making me an offer—and it's more money than I'm making now plus a signing bonus and moving expenses covered. I'm thrilled. I immediately accept and start packing. I'm finally leaving this firm and this city. I'm giving it all to Paul.

Paul was my all. And after the passage of many

many years, I can still say the same thing. As I told the psychiatrist long ago, I just don't connect that well with men.

Despite having a great supportive father, I just never did.

Paul will actually go on to become the head of Litigation in the firm I introduced him to. It's a sweatshop there. So in many ways, I feel like that's the best gift I could have given him. I mean I can't believe he isn't miserable there now. I sure would be.

His wife, as I expected, will never work but will give him two sons with the same jet-black hair he had. I will rock it in Nashville for a time, but it turns out my Dad was right. I am not a Southern girl. I will leave everything I had there and return to Capitol Hill—the only place I have ever belonged.

Silas

When I met Silas, I was only 29 years old.

Today, years later, that seems so young, but then, on the precipice of 30, I felt so old. I soon was exiting my roaring 20s and entering a new decade with strong societal expectations of responsibility, success and child bearing.

Silas was 15 years my senior at 44. Some may ask what in the hell is a 29-year-old girl doing with an almost 45 year old man? But I admired him. He taught me about classical music and how to eat oxtail. He made me run the outer loop of Central Park with him almost every day, even in inclement weather. He took me on Caribbean trips where I learned how to do yoga by the sea. He was a successful businessman with a Harvard MBA and an Upper Westside apartment and a house in the Hamptons.

And he was great in bed.

A year before I had decided to give up my Capitol Hill job and start writing again.

I wanted to use my journalism degree and politics was wearing on me. It seemed like we never got anything done, and I wasn't making a difference after all. I yearned to write, and I had always loved fashion—even more than politics. So I moved to New

York City, the epicenter of fashion, to pursue my dream.

I became an aspiring journalist in the city writing a small column for a reputable fashion magazine. Although I loved my work, I was pretty broke and living in a crap apartment in Chelsea. I loved running and poetry readings and wine tastings. Silas didn't drink much. I have found out pretty quickly that Jews do not drink like WASPs. My family grew up on football, ham and lots of beer. He grew up eating smoked salmon and bagels and drinking Iced Tea. I don't think he ever approved of my drinking and especially because I was at it so often, but back then, I didn't give a shit. I tried to please him in many ways, but I wasn't giving up wine or parties. Silas wasn't into parties like I was. But then I went to a state school where binge drinking was prevalent. Anyway, I would say besides the drinking, we had everything in common.

"Listen to the music," Silas would coach me as we lay in bed drinking pumpkin coffee, "this is the Swan." I would lay in bed naked with sweat trickling between my legs and listen. The violin with its sadness and regret mirrored Silas's moods at times. I could see why he listened to this song so often.

"Today we will run six miles." Silas told me while bundling up, tucking his beige fleece scarf into an oversized black North Face jacket.

"Silas! Come on! It's 24 degrees outside." I protested vehemently.

I knew we *should* do it, but I didn't feel strongly enough. Silas, however, had obsessive-compulsive tendencies. He wouldn't let me eat chips in Mexican restaurants because he felt they were too caloric. He usually showered twice a day. His apartment was immaculate. And running religiously was something that he required of himself and of me. It was non-negotiable. So I went and powered through it. After running (I'm not kidding), he would often want to go to Equinox, his swank gym, and lift weights. Afterwards he would let me have a lavish breakfast of steak and eggs, and then we'd go home and shower and make love.

It's important to note that we *always* used condoms. I was adamant about this. I have really bad luck. Although I was on the pill, I still believed I could get an STD. We talked about my feelings on this topic once, and then we didn't talk about it ever again. We just used them, and Silas didn't seem to mind.

On the weekends, we spent a lot of time with his brother and sister. I loved them, and they were the opposite of my family without the booze, the drama, and all the fighting. His parents, unlike mine, were still together and had just celebrated their 50th anniversary. I was told they were all calm and sophisticated and successful. His sister was a cellist in the New York symphony, and his brother was an accomplished writer. I wanted to be around them. I somehow felt more sophisticated and worldly in their presence.

I never met Silas' parents. They lived in a tony neighborhood outside Phoenix, and all I know is that pushed their kids way too hard.

All of them were home schooled, had to play instruments and get really good grades. They all went to Princeton, Harvard and Yale. His parents had limited means so all the kids got full rides. I always thought that Silas' moods had something to do with his upbringing and shitty parents, but I never said too much. I figured eventually things would get back to normal.

I loved restaurants. And New York City had so many of them. I wanted to try what I thought of as exotic food like Vietnamese, Ethiopian and escargot. Silas was more of a recluse. He hated the noise, the prices and of course the calories.

"Let's go out to Zoe's! I hear their scallops are amazing." I wanted to get out of his apartment and explore the world.

"I don't want to go to that place. The food is overpriced and full of salt. Plus I can make way better scallops for you here." He would state.

I would capitulate. We would (again) eat in. You probably wouldn't have put up with this crap. I didn't think I would either, but I'm the middle child and have always been a people pleaser. Plus I was already so in love with him, and I always feared him leaving me like the ones before. So I did what I had to do to make him happy.

Plus we had a robust sex life and that counted for a lot. Although a lot of men in their 40s can't keep up with you, Silas had a sex drive that rivaled mine. He could do it twice at night and be charged up again in the morning. I'm not kidding.

And he always went down on me and seemed to love it. He had a fantasy of me being with another woman in front of him, which he often talked about when we were in bed. And I indulged him. It kind of turned me on.

But sometimes in the morning, he would cast his

copy of the *New York Times* on the floor while I was pouring over the book review section. He would roll over away from me and curl up in a ball. I felt alone and confused. I got scared. I would gently touch his bare shoulder, and he wouldn't even move.

"What's wrong, baby? " I tried to approach him.

"Nothing. I just don't want to talk." He would wrap the navy quilted blanket tighter around his stomach and roll over to the edge of the bed.

"Do you want me to make some eggs?"

My Italian mother had taught me that food could cure anything.

"No… I just want to be alone. Could you leave for a little bit?" He murmured.

I slid on my black silk nightgown and quietly left the bedroom. I sat in the living room trying to focus on the newspaper, but it was hard to concentrate. Silas didn't have a television. He believed TV's were evil and contributed to the demise of our brains and that we should all be reading more. Although he loved the Jets and football in general, he barely watched it except on those rare occasions when we were out. I sat for what felt like hours wondering what was going wrong all of the sudden—wondering why this loneliness was sneaking up on me again.

Several hours passed. Silas entered the living room in his plaid flannel pajama bottoms and a navy V-neck T-shirt. He looked a lot better.

"Shall we go to brunch?" He calmly asked—as if nothing had happened at all.

"Are you okay??" I asked emphatically.

"Yes. I'm fine. Let's go." And just like that it passed. The mood was up again.

I felt confused and wary. This kept happening. And I didn't know how much more of this I could take.

"Okay, let me get a shower." I shrugged. Quite honestly, I was delighted he wanted to go out to brunch. I couldn't wait for a Mimosa and a big plate of eggs benedict at a fancy restaurant in Tribeca.

The thing about Silas and I was that despite all the passion, we never showered together. I had some body image issues lingering from high school, and I didn't relish the thought of standing naked in front of a man. Any man. Besides, we always used condoms, and those weren't exactly suitable for the shower.

However, on this particular morning, Silas came into the bathroom and slid into the shower with me. He pushed me up again the aqua blue and heather grey tiled wall and spread my legs first pushing his fingers inside of me, and then his cock. He pushed hard inside me as the warm water beat down on my shoulders.

It felt amazing to be so free—exhilarating in fact. But as he left the bathroom first, I started to think about the fact that for the first time we didn't use a condom. This concerned me—a little. But it'd been a year of dating now, and I knew he was clean. I put the worry out of my mine and got ready for brunch.

That morning we had a glorious time. Silas was suddenly in a great mood, and he even skipped his morning run. He took me to a modern restaurant in Tribeca with bright yellow walls, and we split warm banana muffins and crab eggs benedict. I quickly downed two Mimosas, and even Silas had a glass of champagne. He rarely drank, but if he did, it would always be champagne. I felt light and airy from the bubbles, but I started again thinking about the unprotected sex. I told myself to stop it—to enjoy this moment and stop thinking about the future all of the time.

Silas was really big into Transcendental Meditation and was trying to teach me how to follow a mantra and quiet my mind, but it was never easy for me. I always worried about things. After brunch, Silas suggested we go home and take a nap. We hopped in a cab and headed uptown. I have always had a hard time napping, but the booze was making me relaxed and tired. We peeled off our clothes and jumped in bed. I thought for sure Silas would want to have sex before sleeping, but he just rolled over and started breathing heavy, falling into a deep sleep. When he woke up, he didn't feel well and asked me to get him an Advil and some water.

"Do you think it's the champagne?" I pondered. I mean he didn't drink that often.

"No, I just don't feel well. I think I have a fever." I put my hand on his forehead and he was indeed very warm. I handed him the Advil and a glass of water.

"You do feel kind of warm, Sye."

"Yes. I'm suddenly not feeling so great, dear. I think maybe you should go."

"Okay, I feigned a smile. "Do you need anything? I could go get some soup."

"No, no. He touched my hand. "I just think I need to rest."

My heart sunk. I suddenly felt that familiar feeling of being pushed away. I mean what if we were married? Would he just kick me out? I hated being treated like I was some disposable object, yet I didn't know how to say this to him. I simply put on my coat and graciously left.

* * *

The winter was rapidly progressing. It was cold, windy and bleak. Silas was the one thing I looked forward to at the end of the day. New Year's was approaching, and he suggested we go to his house in the Hampton's for the holiday. I always loved going there watching the well-dressed erudite residents bustle around the upscale grocery store and the restaurants, but Silas only wanted that place for the ocean. In the summer, he was an avid swimmer and enjoyed escaping the blazing city for a peaceful quiet place where he could read and swim. He had little interest in society life or the trendy restaurants and bars, which were just a distraction from the peace and solitude the water offered him. I wanted to experience all of it.

I was hoping he would take me somewhere really nice for New Year's Eve. I could drink a lot of champagne and eat lobster and escargot. But Silas suggested we have a romantic night in instead.

"Don't worry. I can cook better lobster than that restaurant you want to go to. I'll pick up some lobster and champagne at the market."

I felt disappointed, but didn't say too much. That evening we went on a long run in the blustering cold and had a quiet evening inside watching the ball drop in the city together. We had sex later, this time also unprotected. I guess we were done with condoms now. I mean we had already done it without them, why continue now? Plus we were in a serious monogamous relationship now. And I trusted him completely.

* * *

After the holiday, we both went back to our routine and life in the city, Silas dealing with all the financial issues plaguing his Fortune 100 Company and me writing short mundane pieces about the latest trends in fashion. We both got busy for a few days, and I started partying with my girlfriends again. I didn't really miss him, but then, I knew I would see him this weekend and I was enjoying the break. On Thursday night, my phone rang at 10:00 p.m. at night.

"Hello?" I picked up my phone.

"Esme?"

"Hi you." It was Silas.

"How's every little thing?" He would often ask me this especially when he called me from overseas business trips.

"Everything is fine. How are you?"

"I'm okay. I'm okay. So listen... there's something I have to talk to you about."

"What's that?" I slipped into my oversized brown leather chair.

"Well... I don't know quite how to say this. So I'll just say it. I have herpes."

My heart dropped to the floor.

"What? What are you talking about?"

"Last week when you were over, I was having flu like symptoms, that often happens before an outbreak, and then I had the outbreak. I have herpes."

I say nothing.

"So you have been exposed. You need to get tested." He stated flatly.

"What are you talking about? How could you not

107

tell me this? You knew how paranoid I was about this kind of thing." I stood up and yelled.

"I'm sorry. I mean it's been under control for years. I take Valtrex, which helps. I didn't expect this to happen."

"How could you do this to me? How could you lie to me?" I burst into tears.

"I'm sorry. I'm really sorry. Call your doctor."

I hang up. There is nothing left to say.

I call my doctor. I have to figure this out. I'm terrified of getting herpes. I'm terrified of getting sick.

"You have to wait 30 days to get tested. Listen, I always tell you girls to use condoms. Herpes is the gift that just keeps on giving."

There is nothing I can do but hope and pray for a month. Pray that nothing happens to me. I hate Silas. How could be put me at risk like this? How could he do this to me? I thought he loved me....

* * *

30 days go by and nothing happens to me. I check myself daily with fear. No redness. No sores. Nothing. I get tested finally. Negative. Thank God.

I also haven't talked to Silas in 30 days. I have had such hatred for him and what he has put me through. I haven't responded to his texts, and we haven't spoken on the phone. Yet, as I can attest after this long month that has just gone by, 30 days is a long time. And despite everything that has occurred, I miss him.

Finally, I decide to return one of his texts. "I'm sorry. Can we talk?"

I write back a simple "Okay."

We decide to meet at a local Mexican restaurant that we both really like. I arrive first and order a bowl-sized margarita with a salt-rimmed glass. I'm going to need it. I'm going to need several.

Silas arrives dressed preppy as always. Dark blue fitted jeans with a navy gingham Brooks Brother dress shirt. Wire rimmed glasses.

"Hello," he pulls the chair out directly in front of me. "It's good to you see."

I take a big gulp out of my drink and say nothing. I just look deeply into his brown eyes.

The waiter comes over to the table with the customary chips and salsa.

"No, no thank you." Silas waves the waiter away.

"Yes. We'll take the chips. Thank you." I grab the basket of chips from the waiter and bite into one. He is *not* controlling this dinner.

"How have you been?" He sips his water. I sip my margarita.

"Stressed. Worried. I mean I doubt you can imagine."

"No, I can imagine. Are you okay?"

"Yes, thankfully I'm okay."

"I'm so glad. Esme…. You don't know how sorry I am."

"It doesn't matter now, does it?" I reach for the chips.

"What can I do to make this better? I love you. I miss you."

"I don't know, Silas. I really do not know."

"I want to start over with you. A fresh start."

I lean my head forward. I'm not sure where this is going.

109

"I know I've mentioned this before, but my boss now is really pushing for me to go to China and run the office there."

"You mentioned it to me."

"Well, I am thinking about it now, but it is a five year assignment."

"Five years?"

"Yes... I want you to go with me."

"What in the hell am I going to do in China? Write for a state-controlled newspaper? Geez Silas. How can you drop this on me now?"

"I'm sorry. I didn't want to bring this up tonight, but they are pressuring me to go. I have to decide soon."

"I can't go to China for five years. I won't even see my family. I'd have to give up my job. What would I do there?"

"You wouldn't have to do anything. You could be an ex pat wife and do whatever you want."

"Oh, I see. I'm just supposed to sit around all day while you are at work. Get my nails done. Go to the gym?"

"There are other ex pat wives there. You will make friends. You will have plenty to do."

"Silas, I just can't handle this right now."

"I know. I know. Just know I love you. Take your time."

* * *

One of my best friend's weddings is coming up in DC next week. Silas and I are going. We're trying. I still love him, and we're trying to put the past behind us. I still don't know about China, but I guess that too is on the table. Last weekend, Silas took me shopping for a new dress for the event. He loved a long black dress with an Asian print on it, so I opted for that one. I preferred a solid chocolate brown dress, but of course, he got his way. I keep thinking I'm going to do what I want to do one of these days, but I never do. It has just become much easier to give in.

Silas and I take the train down to DC. It's very pleasant. He reads a book about Silicon Valley and investing in tech companies—something I've encouraged him to do. I take out my laptop and write a short piece about the comeback of shift dresses. I get a glass of red wine from the food cart in the back of the train, and Silas eats a veggie burger. We go to the back of the train and sit discussing everything—a Senate race, my bitch boss, the Jets, the book he's reading now. We avoid China.

The wedding is a Jewish wedding, and it's going to be lavish at the Mayflower Hotel in the center of DC. We have all of Sunday to explore the city together. There are so many things I want to show him.

Silas and I both love art so we hit the National Gallery of Art and then the Phillips Collection, and he tells me all about the Paul Klee paintings there. He holds my hand gently as we stroll up and down white marble floors looking at beautiful works of art. We go to lunch at an Indian restaurant I love and then take a long walk on the Mall looking at all the memorials. It's a perfect day.

We don't talk about herpes or China or anything that is going to create discord.

We just enjoy each other's company and the scenery—it's actually starting to feel like old times.

111

That night, we attend the wedding. Rachel is in a stunning white sheath dress wearing both diamonds and pearls. There is a chuppah and a glass the groom stomped on on the floor, and people being carried around on top of chairs. I have never been to a Jewish wedding, but it is familiar to Silas and he explains all the rituals to me.

At the reception, I drink *a lot* without reservation and totally let myself go. For once in a long time, I'm having a lot of fun and not thinking at all about the future or being judged. Even Silas is a blast. He drinks champagne and dances with me and my friends. He tells me I'm beautiful and amazing, and I start to think about our wedding one day and how happy I will be.

The next morning we wake up and get room service in bed. We lay there, eating vegetarian omelets, kind of hung over and kind of happy to be away from New York. But Silas's mood suddenly shifts again. He seems sad and distant. I stand up and start getting dressed, as we have to be at the brunch in 30 minutes.

Silas is sitting on the bed still and presses his hand against his face. He looks anguished and stressed.

"What's wrong, babe? Come on. We have to get going." I brush my hair and put on lip-gloss.

"Esme." He says my name slowly and pauses.

"What? I turn around. "What is it?"

"I can't do this. I can't do this anymore…."

"Do what?"

"This relationship. I can't do it anymore." His eyes have tears in them.

"What are you talking about? We just had a great weekend. A great night last night."

"I'm not happy."

"You're not happy? What the fuck Silas? You just asked me to move to fucking China with you!"

"I'm sad and lonely when I'm with you, and I'm sad and lonely when I'm without you. "

I say nothing. What could I say to that? I go to the brunch alone while Silas packs up our things in the hotel room. I try to stay composed putting scrambled eggs from the buffet on my plate. I smile at old friends and wave. I fear the tears welling up in my eyes, and I begin to lose it.

"What is going on with you? Where is Silas?" My attentive friend Lucy asks me. She reaches for my hand. "Esme, what is going on with you?"

"It's over, Lucy. He just broke up with me." I push my face into my hands and start to sob.

"Why? What happened? It seemed like you guys were having a lot of fun last night?"

"I don't know." I bury my hands in my face. "He said he's sad and lonely when he is with me."

"What does that mean?" Lucy places her hand on mine.

"I don't know. I have to go get my stuff."

"Okay, well you can take a cab back to the train station with us. I'll come get you."

"Thanks." I stand up and head to the room. When I get there, my back is packed. Clothes neatly folded and organized, but Silas is gone. I grab my bag and head to the lobby. I will find Lucy and grab a cab.

As I enter the lobby, I see Silas sitting on a yellow wing backed chair. He looks directly at me. I look away and walk the other way frantically searching for Lucy.

113

I have to get out of here.

"Esme! Esme!" I can see Lucy waving to me. "Let's go!"

I rapidly roll my bag across the marble floor heading toward Lucy. Silas starts to follow me. I walk faster.

"Esme, stop. Let me help you with that."

He pulls the bag out of my hand. Lucy stares at him blankly.

"We have a cab." She states and scowls.

I follow Lucy outside into the blustering wind with Silas directly behind me wheeling my bag. Lucy opens the cab door, and Silas holds it open for me and then places my suitcase in the trunk.

Streams of tears roll down my face. Is this goodbye?

I start to shut the door. He pulls it open.

"I love you. I love you." He looks deep into my eyes.

I slam the door shut.

"Please go." I wave my hand at the cab driver.

* * *

I will never hear from Silas again. Despite the good times and my deep love for him, it just wasn't enough. I guess he was more depressed than I ever realized, and I could not help him or make it better.

But in some ways it was a relief. I could finally do the things that I wanted to do and not be controlled by someone else. I started going to wine tastings with my friend Albert, got a new job covering the entertainment industry, and I quit running.

Years later, I will find out that he got married, had a little boy and did in fact move to China. But he wouldn't make the five-year assignment. He was diagnosed with Stage 4 Leukemia and died at the young age of 52. I didn't go to the funeral, but I did send his family a basket of fruits and cheeses. They sent me a thank you note as they realized how much he had once meant to me.

Silas didn't become my husband as I had planned when I was much younger. But despite the lies and betrayal, he left an indelible impression on my heart.

Ezra/Jack

Ezra

The orange light goes off on the phone in my office. Yet again.

I sighed. Another partner. Another legal emergency.

I reluctantly pick it up.

"Hello. This is Esme." I always have a feigned upbeat greeting.

"Oh yeah, this is Bart Fishburne. Can you come down to my office now?"

I throw down my red pen where I had been redlining a contract that is due by close of business. It is 2:00. Just what I needed—another emergency.

I slide on my navy blue patent leather heels and head down the hall with a pen and yellow legal pad in hand to take notes on my next assignment.

"Hello Esme," Bart greets me looking down and rubbing his hands fervently through the stacks of legal documents scattered all over his desk.

"Hello." I sit down quietly in the deep black leather chair directly in front of his desk. This is what you are supposed to do.

"Listen, here's the thing," he reaches across his desk and hands me a stack of legal documents. "Our client, Codo Communications, is merging with a large broadband provider in New York on Friday. It's a $50 million deal, and there could be antitrust implications. I need you to take a look at these documents and file a Hart-Scott-Rodino."

I am taking notes diligently but inside, I'm freaking out. That's only three days away, and I already have a pile of papers on my desk all with immediate deadlines attached to them. I sigh. I'm going to have to cancel dinner with Daniel, a guy I recently start dating, and pull an all-nighter again. I swear. I'm never going to have a boyfriend.

But you can never say no. They view that as insubordination, and it surely jeopardizes your chance of becoming a partner anytime in the near future.

Not that I care so much about partnership these days—but I certainly don't want to get into trouble. Especially with the tyrant Bart Fishbourne—known as the worst partner to work for in Corporate.

Even though corporate law is relatively boring, I picked it because it's more stable and predictable (most days). I never thought I had the guts to litigate, and the schedule is just so unpredictable. The litigators' vacations were always getting cancelled, and opposing counsels were often total assholes that engaged in nonstop dilatory tactics. Not for me. I would take the due diligence, the contract review and the antitrust filings over that nightmare.

Yet the litigators, by nature, were fighters and super cool. All the people in Corporate were total nerds and boring. I didn't really have any friends at the firm in my practice group. So I always found myself two floors below visiting with my litigator friends. We are all associates at a prestigious Nashville law firm, and we are all overworked and tired. We like to take regular breaks in the afternoon to bitch about the workload and make fun of the partners. My best friend there is Anna, and I find myself in her office often eating snacks and bitching with the door closed.

She is cranky by nature but very funny. She is already a top litigator and works primarily for Ezra Rubinstein, the Harvard educated award-winning head of the Litigation department.

Ezra immediately took a liking to me and would often stop by Anna's office during one of our afternoon bitch sessions. Given his interest in my career development, I probably would have thrived in Litigation under his tutelage, but I just couldn't bear the thought of it.

"Hello ladies." He would always say as he stopped by Anna's office. Tall, wiry, and out of style with horn-rimmed tiny glasses. Although he was allegedly a brilliant lawyer, he always looked unkempt.

"Hello Ezra," Anna would smile. She thought he was kind of weird and neurotic, but she knew she had to stay in his good graces or all of the good cases would cease to be given to her.

"Hello Ezra," I smiled feigning enthusiasm, as always, "how are you?"

"I'm good. Just prepping for court tomorrow." He slid into the chair next to me.

"Yes. I'm almost done with the interrogatories. I have a little more work to do on them." Anna attested.

I could see her visibly tensing up. She didn't like it when he stopped by her office and lingered— especially when I was there. I didn't know what that was about. Sometimes I thought she was jealous of the attention he gave me.

"And how is Corporate, Esme?" He pulled down his glasses. "What are you working on?"

"Oh, I just have this contract to review and a Hart-Scott-Rodino to file."

"That sounds very boring to me!" He started to laugh. "You really ought to consider switching to Litigation. I think you would make a great litigator."

"She doesn't want to do litigation. She eschews conflict." Anna interrupted.

"That's not true!" I protested. "I just never thought I'd be good at it."

"Of course you would be. You have the personality—and the brains. Stop by my office later this week. We should talk more." He wiped his runny nose with his index finger and got up and started to leave.

"Okay. I will." I mean what was I going to say to the head of Litigation?

"He's always stopping by when you are in here." Anna was resuming her curmudgeon personality.

"That's not true, Anna. It's you he loves. He loves your briefs!"

"I just wish he wouldn't stop by. It annoys me. Now let's talk about the tyrant. When is your filing due?"

"Friday," I sighed. "It never ends. I'm going to yet again have to cancel my date with Daniel."

"You should. He's a Neanderthal."

Anna married early in life to a darling man who puts up with a lot of her crap. In general, she hates most men. She particularly hated the men I dated and thought they were not worthy of me. She never had an appreciation of how hard it is to be single and how much crap you really did have to put up if you wanted a boyfriend. Daniel was sweet and paid for everything and sometimes brought me flowers. However, he may have been a meathead. He was a former college football player and loved sports, which I loathed. He also had a very mediocre job in an accounting firm and never read the newspaper or books. Quite honestly, besides the sex and the occasional fun dinner out, we had little in common. But I was lonely and bored at the firm, and seeing him was something to look forward to at night.

"You're a snob, Anna. He is a super nice guy— just because he isn't a lawyer or doctor!"

"Does he read anything at all? I mean what do you guys talk about?"

"That's it!" I exclaimed. I am getting more irritated by the minute. I'm leaving!"

* * *

That week I continued to slog away on my tedious Hart-Scott-Rodino antitrust filing. It was very stressful as a lot was riding on this. If we didn't do it right, the companies would not be able to merge, and I'm sure my firm would be fired for fucking it up. The partners never gave you much guidance because they were too busy themselves. As such, this whole thing was riding on me, and I had no idea what the fuck I was doing. After lunch, I grew tired and bored. I needed a break and decided to head downstairs to the Litigation floor. But this time I walked past Anna's office and into Ezra's. I mean he *had* told me to stop by later in the week to discuss my career.

Anna is a negative person in general, and I didn't want to hear her opinion on Daniel again. I mean I knew he wasn't Mr. Right, but I was fine with him being Mr. Right Now until I found the right one. Paul and I had broken up eight months ago and despite moving to a new city and changing my life, I was still devastated by it and on the rebound. I felt like I needed a boyfriend to keep my mind off things and also to get back at him. Quite honestly, I don't even know if he would care if he did find out, but I wanted to hurt him as much as he had hurt me. Plus, if truth were told, I think I may have been the type of girl who always needed male attention because I always felt like I wasn't good enough for most things. Somehow when men (versus women) paid me compliments, I felt a lot better.

"Hello!" I acted chipper and friendly as I slowly walked into his office. I was glad that finally someone was taking an interest in my career, and I wanted to impress him.

I was fashionable and always wore high stylish heels and straightened my hair perfectly. I wore chic black Diane von Furstenberg wrap-a-round black dresses instead of navy blue Ann Taylor suits. I realized that I stood out, but I kind of liked being different than the other boring lawyers. I liked the compliments that I frequently got about my shoes and dresses, but maybe I was pushing the envelope a bit. Anna, a true conservative, definitely had her opinions on that.

"Hello Esme! I'm so glad you stopped by!" Ezra exclaimed.

"Well you said stop by later in the week so I am." I smiled.

"I love those shoes. You look great today!"

Ezra's office was three times the size of mine and faced the water. Despite his crappy ties and worn out suits, his office was amazing. He had modern leather furniture and expensive abstract art on his walls. There was one picture on his desk of his attractive (much younger) wife and three grown kids and a copy of *The Economist*. He had both his Williams and Yale degrees displayed right above his desk for easy view and photos with senators and city officials on the adjacent wall. He had a big black globe, which Anna said he liked to spin in serious meetings. I was really impressed and was just hoping one day I'd be as successful as him. I was kind of hoping he would take me under his wing and teach me how to be a brilliant lawyer like him. I knew I wasn't a very good lawyer right now but was hopeful that one day I would be.

"How are things? How goes your filing? Have a seat." He motioned to the low black leather seat directly next to him. Most partners sat behind their desks and summoned you to the chair in front of them, but Ezra believed in equality, and I think he was trying to make me fill more comfortable and less intimidated.

"It's going." I sighed. "It's kind of boring. And I'm not even sure I'm doing it right."

"Oh, I'm sure you are doing a great job, Esme." He smiled.

"I doubt it. I mean it's not like they teach you how to do it."

"Well, Bart is a little prickly I know, but he sure brings in a lot of business. What you need is a mentor. Law firms can be difficult places to navigate."

He reached for his coffee mug with the law firm named printed on it.

"Can I get you anything to drink?"

He has a small refrigerator in his office, and I knew for a fact they stocked those things with wine and beer for the late nights.

"No, no. I'm fine. Yes, I guess you're right. It would be nice to have a mentor. I really like Juliet, but she's so busy lately." Juliet was a senior associate. She gave me a ton of work in health care mostly, but she never had time to talk or have lunch.

"Well, consider it done! I will be your mentor." He slammed his coffee cup on the silver end table.

"Really? I mean do you have the time?" I was shocked and kind of flattered.

"I'll make the time! Plus, I still think you'd be a great litigator. We need to work on that."

I laughed. "Okay. Okay. I'll consider it."

"Well, what are you doing this evening? Let's grab a drink after work!"

"Oh I can't. The Hart-Scott-Rodino filing is due tomorrow, and I have a lot of work to do tonight." I would have done anything to skip this banal project and have a drink with Ezra, but there was no way I could get out of this now.

"Okay, I'll take a rain check." He stood up and put on his gray torn jacket. "I have to be in court in 15 minutes." He picked up his briefcase and shook my hand.

"Okay, thanks again." I smiled.

"You got it! And... think about what I said."

"Okay, I will." I started thinking a lot about switching to litigation. I wasn't sure I could do a deposition. I'm not great on my feet. I certainly knew I couldn't go to a jury trial. I just wasn't confident enough even if I was sitting second chair.

But I'd have Ezra mentoring me and teaching me new things. He was the only one who seemed to care about my career development here, and I was really grateful for his help.

* * *

Although I was still in Corporate, over time, Ezra and I started to spend a lot of time together. He could do anything. He showed me the key items to look for in due diligence and edited all my letters to clients making them much better. He took me out to fancy lunches at the best restaurants, and we talked about everything—his kids, law school, his cases, my dismal dating life and my sadness about lingering sadness about Paul. He built me up and told me I was special and could have anyone I wanted. He told me one day I'd be a fantastic lawyer with many clients.

Law firm life became more cheerful. I at least had a friend as Anna had started to distance herself from me. During the days, I felt pretty good with all the mentoring and compliments. Finally, my grave insecurities about being a lawyer were starting to dissipate. I felt like I was writing better and even starting to "get it."

Late at night, after work, I would feel sad and lonely.

I would come home and open a bottle of wine, skip dinner, and light a cigarette and then another and lay on my plush pine velvet couch staring at the ceiling praying to God that this feeling would pass. I never felt like eating and had skipped the running I used to do all the time.

125

But the days were better. I still had trouble getting out of bed in the morning, but work was getting easier as I got better and more efficient. Ezra stopped by almost every afternoon to give me a pep talk too. Anna, however, told me that some of the partners were starting to get concerned about it. He was always on my floor, two floors up from Litigation, and the partners in Corporate I guess thought he had no business being on my floor all the time. I ignored her bitter comments. I didn't care what these nosy people thought, and I figured she was just jealous that he was mentoring me not her. Plus, like I said, he was making me a better lawyer, and that's all that mattered.

* * *

One late afternoon evil Bart summoned me to his office. I walked over filled with dread knowing this was going to be another brutal assignment with a tight deadline. Another all-nighter. It turned out that I had to review a lot of contracts and look for key provisions in a hospital acquisition with a 24-hour turnaround time. As I got back into my office slumping in my chair, tired and anxious, I saw the orange light on my phone. It was Ezra. I picked it up.

"Hello lady!" He always seemed to be in a great mood. "Whatcha doing?"

"Just started due diligence." I sighed. "Another last minute assignment from Bart."

"Oh, that's unfortunate. I was hoping we could grab a drink at five."

"Oh, I wish. I'll be here all night I'm sure."

"Well that blows. Okay then…. good luck."

I was bummed. I somehow always hoped that the powerful rainmaker Ezra would save me from evil Bart, but then I knew there was no way one partner would ever go against another—especially when that partner brought in a lot of clients like Bart did. I decided to suck it up. I went into the break room and made a big cup of coffee instead of my customary evening red wine. I just wanted to be home alone. I really needed a cigarette.

I started to pour through the contracts, documenting the questionable provisions in a memo to Bart. I was growing tired and distracted by my phone, but I knew I had to toil through it tonight. Three hours passed, and I still had 20 contracts to go through.

Suddenly, I heard a knock at my door. It was Ezra. I looked at my watch. It was almost 9:00. He never stayed this late.

"Hi, can I come in?" He stood at my door waiting for the invitation to enter.

"Yes." I didn't want to be rude, but I really didn't have time to chit hat.

"Thanks." He shut my door. I kind of thought this was weird. I mean he never shut my door or his door when we spoke. At my law firm, everyone had an open door policy.

"There's something I need to talk to you about"

"Okay." I put my red pen down.

"It's kind of personal though, but I need to talk to you about it."

"Okay," I was getting a little bit concerned. I wasn't sure what this personal matter was, but I also wasn't quite sure why he was talking to me about it.

"Well, the thing is I've been having chest pains…."

"Chest pains? Are you okay? Did you see a doctor? I leaned forward.

"Yes, I did. I saw a cardiologist. I thought maybe I was having a heart attack, but it wasn't that.

"Well, what was it? What is wrong?" I grew concerned. He was 62, and that's often when things start to go wrong. I hoped it wasn't anything serious.

"Well, the thing is. I have been lactating."

My heart dropped. What the fuck? And why was he telling me this?

"Lactating?"

"Yes, it turns out I have too much estrogen. The doctor doesn't know why, but he had to give me testosterone pellets... they insert them in your hip."

I stared straight ahead.

"But the thing is, I'm so horny. I can't stop thinking about sex. Even when I go to lunch, I can't help turning my head and looking at women."

"Well…" I paused. I had no idea what to say, and I was increasingly feeling uncomfortable. "Maybe they just gave you too much testosterone."

"And my wife…. I mean she doesn't want to have sex. We haven't had sex for years."

I stared straight ahead. This was getting weird. I just wanted him to leave my office but had no idea how to make that happen.

"The thing is Esme… I can't stop thinking about you. I think about you all the time."

I continue to say nothing.

"It's getting increasingly difficult for me to be around you." He continued.

"Ahm," I pause not quite sure what to do. "I think this is kind of weird. I actually have a lot of work to do. I think maybe you should leave."

"Oh! Okay, he blushed and appeared flustered, "I'm sorry. I'm sorry to bother you with all of this."

"It's okay." I sink my head into my hands.

"I just needed someone to talk to about it with. Okay." He stands up. "Ah, sorry about this. I'll let you get back to work."

* * *

The next day I came to work in a funk—still in shock about what happened last night. I walked rapidly to the Corporate floor trying to avoid Ezra. I fear he will stop by again, but he doesn't. All of this is overwhelming me, and I feel like I need to tell someone about it. I think about going to Anna, my friend and confidante, but she hasn't been so nice to me these days, and she may not believe me anyway given her admiration of Ezra. I think of telling my boss, Juliet, but she's out of the office with client meetings most of the day, and I don't want to bug her with this. I decide it's best to do nothing. I decide it's best to just lay low. I mean I'm just some low level second year associate. Who's going to believe me? And Ezra brings in a ton of business. *No one* is going to do anything to him.

A month goes by and still no contact with Ezra. He doesn't stop by anymore, and I never go to his floor. Things become banal and boring again in Corporate. I get more last minute grueling assignments, but this time I have no one to talk to about it or even go out to lunch with in the afternoon. I feel lonely and isolated at work just like I do at home. And despite Ezra's inappropriate behavior, I kind of miss him.

On February 14th, I go to work late as usual. It's Valentine's Day—a particularly sad day for me because once again I don't have a boyfriend. I already see roses on my women colleagues' desks, and I just know I won't be getting any flowers this year.

I have just broken up with Daniel. It was kind of mutual really, but I could no longer handle the obsession with college football and our endless conversations about nothing. Maybe I should have kept him around to Valentine's Day though. I think about what Paul is doing with his new love, and my heart sinks.

Then my secretary comes in my office and drops a large beige inter-office envelope on my sloppy desk covered with marked up papers. I have no idea who this could be from, but I'm afraid. Maybe it's a formal reprisal from Bart or a notice that I'm getting fired for doing a crappy job on the antitrust filing. But I know I have to open it. I slowly untie the cord that covers the top of it. I open it and pull out a homemade Valentine's Day card.

It's childlike. Pale pink construction paper on a white doily in the shape of a heart. And there it is—a handwritten poem written and signed by Ezra. The sentences rhyme with a perfect cadence. He writes about my beautiful flowing hair, my big eyes and my bright smile. I simply can't believe it. He's actually signing his name to it. I quickly slip it into the envelope not quite sure knowing what to do with it.

Then the orange light on my phone goes off. It's Ezra. I don't know what to do, but we often do stupid things when we are in shock. I pick it up.

"Good morning, Esme."

"Hello."

"So I was just wondering... did you get my Valentine?"

"Yes, it just came."

"I was wondering what you thought."

"I don't know. It's kind of strange."

He says nothing.

"Listen, I have to go." I rapidly hang up the phone and bury my head in my hands trying to decide what to do next.

I decide to call Anna. This time I have concrete evidence, and I know I need to tell someone.

I pick up the phone. She answers on the first ring.

"Hey… can you come up here?"

"Well, I'm working on a brief now. How about we talk later?"

"Can you just come up now? It's important."

"Okay. I'm coming."

When Anna arrives, I hand her the Valentine. I then tell her about the late night conversation and the lactating. She first is shocked, and then she is very angry.

Anna is an ardent feminist, and she doesn't put up with bad male behavior. I mean I also am into women's issues but not like her. She tells me she is going to tell Kyle—a young partner in her group that she is fond of and trusts. He's one of the good guys.

I am scared. I do *not* want him to know. He's very respected litigation partner. I just know he will do something. I don't want any trouble.

However, I should have known better. After Anna leaves my office, she runs directly into Kyle's. She tells him everything.

131

"I am not surprised about Ezra. He's a creep. But this is outrageous." Kyle tells her.

"I know. I know." Anna agrees. "We have to do something. We have to talk to her."

"Is she really not going to do anything about this? This is a smoking gun. The jackass signed his name to the Valentine."

"I don't know what she will do, but she's got to report this to management."

After about an hour, Anna returns to my office, this time with Kyle.

"Listen lady. This isn't just inappropriate—this is outrageous. This is sexual harassment, and this type of behavior is just not tolerated at this firm." Kyle's voice is raised.

I stare at him blankly.

"You need to report this to management. Jack Meadow would never put up with this crap."

"They'd probably give you a big settlement to shut the fuck up, Esme. They certainly don't want this getting out to the public." Anna chimes in.

"I don't want a settlement, Anna. Nothing happened."

"Nothing happened? This *is* sexual harassment. And if you don't do anything about it, it's just going to happen to another woman."

I start to think about that and realize she has a valid point. But I'm scared to do anything. Ezra is very powerful here and a rainmaker. I am nothing to them. Nothing.

"Think about." Kyle says as he starts to exit my office. "I mean really think about this, Esme."

* * *

I do think about it and often. But I'm actually okay. I'm a strong woman, and I can get over this just like I got over the break up with Paul. In retrospect, I realize I was very young—only 27—and very naïve. It was sexual harassment, and I should have reported it.

Years later, after I left the firm, I find out that he did, in fact, do it to another woman. She, however, did report it, and I guess she got a settlement to be quiet. I always felt bad about that. I mean if I had reported it, it probably never would have happened to her. In fact, I'm sure it wouldn't have. But I just didn't have the courage or the strength to face those at the top at that age.

* * *

Jack

10 years later

I have just started a plum job as the Legislative Director to a very popular and prominent U.S. Senator from Idaho. I am shocked I even got it as I didn't go to Harvard, and I didn't have any connections. But I was climbing Capitol Hill rapidly due primarily to lots of hard work and I think, good political instincts. Politics unlike law came easy to me, and I was always good at negotiating and striking deals which is really what it was all about there. The goal was always to get a bill to the Senate floor for a vote and to garner 60 votes to get it enacted. I was pretty good at that.

133

This time though I was the Legislative Director, the number two position in the office, only second to the Chief of Staff who rarely did much work. The vast majority of the Chiefs were old white men that just happened to be besties with the senator.

It was very difficult for a woman to have this top position, and I never aspired to get it really. I saw the glass ceiling early on. The Legislative Director, usually a woman, really does all the work and is responsible for managing a staff of immature and competitive legislative assistants as well as every piece of legislation of interest to the senator. There was no way to really advance.

I was always the first one in at 8:00 a.m. and the last one out usually at 8:00 p.m. I was grossly underpaid but always grateful to have the job. I knew 100 people stood at the front door coveting my position so I couldn't fuck up.

The problem was though, I had a very difficult relationship with the Chief of Staff. It was not this way early on, of course, but as time went by, it became increasingly challenging to deal with him on a daily basis. And I knew for a fact that everything I said or did was reported by him directly to the Senator—of course his version of the situation. I started to grow increasingly paranoid and worried that the senator wasn't going to like me anymore either. But I knew there really was little I could do about it.

Jack Davenport, our feared and revered Chief of Staff, was a brilliant man. I'll give him that much. He was a great writer, a strong advocate, and possessed keen political instincts. He certainly didn't put up with any shit from the Republicans even though they were constantly trying to fuck us over. His job though wasn't to deal with the Hill much. His job was to get the Senator reelected. This meant he had to do something he loathed—go to fundraisers. Jack liked to leave by 6:00 to have cocktails with the other Chiefs and corporate lobbyists with expense accounts. The last thing he wanted to do was give up his evenings to beg people for money so he sent me out to do this—on top of all my work. I didn't mind it so much as I liked meeting new people and collecting business cards for the Senator. I figured the overtime I was willing to put in might compensate for my reputation, which I feared was growing worse by the day thanks to Jack.

When Jack wasn't drinking and yelling at me, he was writing a book about Senate procedure. It was an arcane topic but one that would interest those inside the Beltway. He spent countless hours of his day writing this book all on the taxpayer dime. I didn't dare question him about this—nor did anyone—including the senator. But it seemed really unfair to me, and I was growing tired of doing all the work.

Jack had a huge temper and scared the shit out of the staff. On Memorial Day weekend, when all the young staffers had plans to hit the Delaware beaches, he made me tell them that not all of them could go away only days before the weekend.

When I refused to do it, he told me I had to do it by the end of the day. I offered to cancel my plans to Maine with my boyfriend, but he said it had to be one of the legislative assistants to stay in the office and answer the phones. This was one of the toughest days I can remember. And only two volunteered to do it. The others were fed up and threatened to quit. But alas, we had two, and they would stay to do nothing else but man phones that would never ring.

The other thing about Jack was that he was bipolar. Some days he would scream at me, and some days he would complement me usually about my outfits or my appearance. Occasionally, he would invite me to go to the very private and exclusive Senator's dining room and say inappropriate things to me. One day he invited me to go with him for a private lunch allegedly to discuss his book, which he told me I *had* to read. I didn't want to go as I hated being alone with him, but this really wasn't an invitation you could decline.

We walked into the dining room, and immediately I spotted a lot of white heads—mostly old Senators and their old Chief of Staffs, and Jack waved at them. They all knew him. I, in a snug red dress, stood out like a sore thumb and when heads turned, I felt really uncomfortable. I just knew I did not belong there and maybe not in the Senate in general.

Jack handed me the tall brown menu that had all kinds of fancy food on it. I automatically gravitated to the fish of the day, salmon, and knew that was what I would order. I really wanted their famous crab cakes but knew they had way too much mayonnaise, and I was desperately trying to keep my weight down. I couldn't run anymore due to my crazy hours so I had to manage my weight through my diet. Jack, who I forgot to mention had quite the belly, ordered a cheeseburger and fries and a glass of Sancerre. I couldn't imagine drinking at lunch especially in front of U.S. Senators, but this is how he rolled. He was just invincible, and he knew it.

He looked up from his menu and placed his bulky black glasses on the white tablecloth. I felt him looking at me up and down.

"I like that dress, Esme. It's really cool, but a bit short, don't you think?" At 5'9", there wasn't a dress that hit my knees directly, but this one was barely above my knees and I was careful to cover my legs with thick black tights.

"I don't know. I thought it was okay." I was shocked and didn't know how to respond. I could feel my face get red and my palms start to sweat.

"Well, I like it. It looks very nice on you." The waitress set down the wine, and he took a huge gulp.

"Thanks." I sipped my ice water slowly and looked around the room. It was always interesting to see who was there, and I preferred to look at them versus him.

"So, have you had a chance to look at my book?"

"Well, I've been so busy with work..."

"You haven't read any of it?" His voice was getting louder.

"Well, I read some."

"What did you think? Do you think it is helpful to Senate staffer?"

"Oh, definitely." I lied. It was a stupid boring book, and no one would buy it.

"Those are *all* your thoughts?" He stared deeply into my eyes.

"I think I just need to dive into it. I will try to this weekend."

"You need to balance your work more, Esme. And reading is a part of your job."

"I will take a look at it when I'm in Idaho next week."

During the weeklong Senate breaks, I wasn't in DC coasting like everyone else. I was expected to go to Idaho and meet with constituents and attend more fundraisers with the Senator. In sum, wherever he went, I went, and the pace was just nonstop. I craved the solitude of my apartment and catching up on all my reading over the recess, but I was a senior policy advisor and expected to make the trips across the country on regular basis.

"You know. You are very hot. I'll give you that. But I question the brains part."

I said nothing. I started to feel like I was going to jump out of my skin, but I bit my lip firmly.

"What's going on with the climate change bill? Do you have the votes?" He looked at his watch.

"Well, last I checked, we were at 41."

"Forty-one?"

"Maybe 42, if we get Robinson. He's on the fence right now."

"What the fuck?" He took another big gulp of his wine and then ordered another.

"We have problems with the Republicans. You know that many of them do not believe we even have a climate change problem."

"Well convince them. Didn't you get the data on the science from Duke?"

"Yes, I've been in contact with them daily, and so has Hadley's office. We're working on it together."

"Well, don't let Hadley's office lead for Christ sakes. You're the lawyer, and this is our bill."

"Okay. I will." I hated the obsequious behavior I was exhibiting, but I knew I had to pacify him or I would be subject to another rage.

"And tonight we have drinks at the Hamilton hotel at 6:00. I want you to be there. We're going to meet with the energy lobbyists. I need to get them on board. Actually you need to get them on board."

I always dreaded drinks with Jack. Don't get me wrong. I loved red wine and drank a lot of it with my girlfriends, but I didn't want to spend my evenings with him, and I hated the way he acted when drinking.

"Well, I think we have votes late tonight. I may need to be on the floor."

"Fuck the floor. Get Jim to cover it." Jim was a solid legislative assistant who covered telecommunication issues, but he was also Jack's chauffeur and personal assistant. Jim, like the rest of us, would do whatever Jack said.

"Okay. I'll talk to him. I'll be there."

At 5:00 p.m. that day, Jack got up to leave the office. It was an unspoken rule that I would be glued to my phone all night getting updates from the Senate floor keeping him apprised. He barely responded when I texted him or if he did, it would just be "ok," but I was still required to be in constant communication with him. It wasn't shocking to me that he was leaving early. He came and went as he pleased, and I knew that by 5:00 he was jonesing for a drink.

"See you in an hour." He peeked his head into my office directly next to his. "Hamilton Hotel."

I don't think Jack ever went home earlier than 10:00 or 11:00 at night. His wife was still in Idaho raising his two young girls, and as far as I could tell, he had nothing to do with them. It was common knowledge that she (just like the Senator's wife) was just collecting the paycheck and the pension and wanted nothing to do with him or DC. Everyone thought he was having an affair, but I just couldn't imagine anyone wanting to sleep with him. Fat, pushing 64, and full of vitriol. I just couldn't imagine it, but then as they say, in DC, power in an aphrodisiac, and he certainly had a lot of power.

At 5:45 pm, I left the office, hailed a cab and headed to the Hamilton. I texted my boyfriend and let him know that again I couldn't see him. It seemed I never could make solid plans on the weekdays. He was a well-known handsome tech lobbyist who I met when working on the House side, and he liked lavish meals and cocktails. I knew he was getting annoyed with my schedule, and I always feared he would dump me. Just like my job, there were plenty of women waiting to fill my place.

I walked into the back of the Hamilton, which was private, and Jack was sitting alone in the back at a quiet booth.

"Sit down." He summoned me. "What do you want to drink?"

"Um, I'll have the house Cab." I just knew either he was paying for this with campaign funds or the lobbyists would pick up the large tab—both of which made me uncomfortable. I wasn't sure this was legal, but I knew it was certainly unethical. But Jack never ever paid for anything with his own money.

"I ordered some calamari and truffle fries.'" He started to munch on the cocktail nuts on the table. I loved calamari and found it so hard to resist especially when I was drinking. It always annoyed me that he had to order all this junk food followed by a big meal. But I knew I could stay strong. I had to save up my calories for the wine. I knew I was going to be here for a while.

"What's going on on the floor?" He leaned in toward me.

"Not much. They have a cloture vote but not until 9:00. Joe is on the floor with the Senator. He'll keep me posted."

"Good. I'm glad to see you are finally on top of it."

"I don't think the Republicans are going to vote to invoke cloture though."

"Where did you get that information?"

"The whip's office." I stated firmly. I mean this was the most reliable source.

"Oh, that's bullshit. Douglas never knows what the fuck is going on."

He would always ask me question about the pending legislation and what was going on on the Senate floor. But then when I told him what I knew which I knew to be true, he would discredit me—as if I was lying. This made me never want to tell him anything, but he was a control freak and was always asking me for updates.

"I don't know, Jack. That's what I was told."

My Cabernet finally arrived, I found myself drinking it too rapidly. It tasted really good, I felt stressed and just wanted to numb myself. I noticed the lobbyists hadn't arrived and began to wonder where they were. They were usually the first to arrive with credit cards and talking points.

"Where are the energy lobbyists?" I looked at my watch.

"Oh, they had to cancel. Fundraisers tonight or something. We're going to reschedule for next week."

I began to wonder why the fuck I was even there. I could have been with my boyfriend having sushi at Mezzanine followed by mind-blowing sex, but instead I was stuck here with this megalomaniac.

"Anyway, we need to talk about the election. We're in cycle now and have only eight months to get our shit together. And I think we may have a primary with this liberal fuck who is going to try to attack us on the environment if we don't get this fucking climate change bill passed."

I just nodded my head. I had no idea why he was talking to me about the campaign because he never had before. He and the Senator and four other old white men would have their summits in Sun Valley to go over campaign strategy. I was never invited. In fact, they never even told me what was discussed.

"You need to get this bill to the floor and passed, Esme. Do you understand the importance of this?"

I felt my chest tighten, and I started to grind my teeth. There was nothing I could do to control the Senate. It was always chaos and gridlock and backstabbing. I had no idea how I was going to get the additional votes. I knew I had to pull in the New England Senators, but I wasn't sure even then we could pass the bill.

"I understand."

"We need two more!" Jack motioned to the waitress as he dug into the calamari and chugged his wine. I think he was already on his third or fourth glass. And the more he drank, the weirder things got.

"So how is that boyfriend, Esme?" Our office was small and Machiavellian. Everyone liked to gossip about everyone else. I knew Jack knew about Evan.

Like I said, Evan was kind of well known on Capitol Hill.

"He's fine. Busy." I started again to feel uncomfortable. And the calamari in front of me began to look more and more inviting.

"I don't know why you go out with that ass. He's just another one of those slimy lobbyists that is always trying to sneak something into a bill."

Most of the lobbyists did have pretty bad reputations in DC, but they funneled money into the campaigns so the Senators needed them. It was a symbiotic relationship, which had seemed to work well for many years. For a lobbyist though, Evan was pretty well respected. He had previously served as a technology lawyer for Microsoft and had even argued a patent case before the Supreme Court. He lobbied on fairly respectable things like immigration reform and health information technology. I didn't have a problem with it, and with his big salary, he showered me with gifts and a summer beach house. I felt very lucky to be dating him.

"I don't think he's that way. He's mostly lobbying on tech issues."

"Whatever, Esme. Boy, are you naïve…. When do you go to Idaho again?"

"My flight is next Sunday."

"I don't like it when you are away from me…. it really disrupts my life."

I had no words for this. I had no idea why he was saying these things. It didn't seem like this meeting was work related at all.

"I thought you wanted me in Idaho."

"Well, the Senator does. But I like it better when

143

you are here. I like having my drinking buddy around."

"I need to meet with constituents and make sure we are solid on our issues. The Latinos aren't happy about our immigration bill."

"Oh, fuck them. They're never happy. We have law enforcement on our ass on border security, and we don't need a hit from the right this year."

I was told to work on immigration reform with a liberal Democrat and to make sure the Hispanic community could support the legislation. Now he was telling me to fuck them and put in more border security provisions. I never knew which way I was supposed to go because he was so bipolar. This is another reason I always feared I would be fired.

"I guess I should be going." I wanted to get the hell out of there and was hoping I still had a little bit of time left to see Evan.

"One more drink." He sipped the last drop of his white wine.

"Jack, I have to be up early tomorrow. I really should go."

"Why don't you come back to my apartment? We can have a night cap there."

This was a new thing. He had never invited me back to his apartment, and now I knew exactly where this was going.

"I don't think that's a good idea."

I decided at this point I had to stand up for myself. But again, I had no idea what he would tell the Senator about me tomorrow. He may even tell him I didn't want to go to Idaho just because *he* didn't want me going.

"It's not like I'm going to molest you, Esme."

"I don't think it's appropriate, Jack."

"Well, I was just inviting you because I have a nice bottle of Chatenauef-du-Pape I was waiting to open up. I know how you love the red."

"I really need to get some sleep. I'll see you tomorrow." I stood up and rapidly rushed to the front door and hailed a cab.

When I got home, I called Evan and told him everything that had happened.

"That fuck. What a total jackass. You need to shut this down, Esme." He screamed at me over the phone then took a drag of his cigarette.

"What am I supposed to do about it? Do you know what he can do to me? He has the Senator's ear. They meet every single morning before work."

"Fuck it. Quit. You can get a better job in the private sector anyway. You need to start making some money."

"I can't quit. That's not even possible."

"Yes. Yes. You can." I could hear him taking another drag of his cigarette.

"I'm not quitting!" I was not a quitter. I loved the issues I worked on and felt like I was really making a difference in the world. I could handle Jack. I could get this under control.

"Well, then you need to get a lawyer. Go see the Senate lawyer and get this guy under control."

"I can't do that, Evan. He'll retaliate. He will get me fired."

"Well. Stop having drinks with him. You're opening up the door. Part of this is your fault for going out and drinking with the guy."

"Do you realize that I have to? That it is actually a part of my job?"

"Well, I don't know what more to say. You're hell bent on staying there so you're going to have to figure it out."

I hung up the phone. Now even Evan was blaming me.

* * *

The next day as usual I arrived an hour earlier than everyone else. I had to walk through the Senator's open office to get to mine, and he was always there first reading seven or eight newspapers. Depending on the press coverage that day, we'd know what kind of day we would have. He was obsessed with the news, particularly the news about him, which could be very complimentary or extremely derogatory. You just never knew which way it would go. And if the headlines were bad, his mood would follow. And the whole way things might go a different was is if Meet the Press called asking him to go on the Sunday show.

"Good morning Senator." I smiled as I walked through his office. I was feeling lethargic from all of the drinks and stressed to see Jack, but I had to fake it.

"Morning." He sipped his coffee and didn't look up. I was increasingly aware that he didn't really even like me anymore. He barely acknowledged my presence. I could only imagine what Jack was telling him about me.

I quietly entered my office and turned on my computer trying very hard not to look at Jack, but his office with big glass walls was right next to mine.

I knew that day was going to be particularly rough as the energy bill was going to the floor. We had always been a thorn in leadership's side on the energy issue. The Democrats all liked the alternative energy provisions as well as the subsidies for ethanol. But our senator saw too many special interest provisions in there especially some that were snuck in to protect the coal burning utilities. He had threated to hold up the entire bill unless certain things were taken out. Because the issue was very important to him, so was his floor statement. Our energy legislative assistant, Jill, was supposed to have written something very good over the weekend. She knew the bill was on the floor today, and she knew how important this was.

"Good morning, Jill." I walked over to her cubicle. "How goes the statement? All ready?"

"Almost." I saw that she was still writing it. Fervently typing and stressing.

"Can I read it?" It was my job to review and edit everything before it went to Jack. Jack would then spend hours editing and fixing every word. He considered himself the absolute best writer, and absolutely everything had to go through him before it went to the senator.

"I'm almost done. I'll bring it over to you soon. "She continued to type rapidly.

"Well... I thought you wrote this over the weekend Jill? I mean we're probably going to the floor in two hours, and you know Jack has to look at it."

She stops typing and looks at me directly without fear or concern.

"Well, my college friends rented a cabin in West Virginia this weekend. It was sort of a reunion, so I went."

147

Just like that. She didn't care, and she didn't fear reprisal. That was the thing about these fucking kids I had to manage. They really didn't care, but I would get blamed for the statement not being ready. It was somehow my job to control them even though none of them listened to me. I wasn't much older than they were so I don't think I commanded a lot of respect, and my management style was mellower. They didn't fear me at all. But they should have feared Jack.

"Bring it to me when it's done." I said firmly and walked out of the room. I was getting increasingly stressed as I knew Jack would wig out if he didn't have it soon, but there was nothing I could do.

As I walked back into my office, Jack was standing there and started pacing as he often did.

"So where is the statement, Esme? Have you edited it yet?"

"No. Jill is still working on it. It will be ready soon."

"Still working on it? What the fuck? We're going to the floor in less than two hours."

"I know. I thought she finished this over the weekend."

"She didn't?"

"No."

"Jesus. It's your job to manage these kids. Tell her this thing needs to be done ASAP. Three pages. Six minute speech. Two minutes per page. No more."
"Okay."

I rushed back over to Jill.

"Jill, where are we on this? Jack wants to see it. We're running out of time."

I wanted to strangle her. I knew she would fuck this up, and I would get blamed.

"Almost there." She continued to type.

"It can only be three pages." I told her.

"Printing it now." She rushed over to the printer. "Here… here it is." It was four pages. I said nothing. I took it from her hands and wondered how I was going to whittle this down to three pages.

I took a deep breath and sat down at my desk calmly with a red pen and started marking up the document. It was a piece of crap, and I had limited time to shave off a whole page.

Suddenly, as I was starting the fourth page, Jack stormed into my office.

"Give it to me."

"I'm almost done. Give me five minutes." There was no way I could let him see it in this condition.

"I said give it to me." He grabbed the pages out of my hand and went back into his office.

"Jesus Christ. Didn't I say three pages? We only have six minutes!" He screamed at me through the open door.

"I'll call the floor and ask for more time." I said trying to appease him. I was always trying to find a solution and manage his temper.

He ran out of his office and screamed at me again. "FIX IT!" I turned to face him and he threw the three pages at me directly hitting me in the face. I wiped my face and felt the tears welling up. But I had to hold them back and focus now.

I got on my computer and started deleting then adding words rapidly. I felt tightness at my chest and an inability to focus.

As I got to page two, Jack came back into my office and stood directly over my shoulder staring at my computer as I typed.

149

"Come on. I need it. We're going to the floor."
He yelled in my ear.

"It's not done. It just needs a little more work." I
kept typing trying to ignore him hovering over me.

"Email it to me. NOW." He screamed.

So I did.

Jack ran back into this office, lit a cigarette and
started pounding on his computer. We were no longer
allowed to smoke in federal buildings, but Jack did
whatever he wanted to do. No one—not the Senator —
not the Capitol Hill police—was going to tell him what
to do. I often fantasized about reporting him to the
police who would be forced to make the smoking stop,
but I didn't think that was such a good idea because he
would definitely find out it was me.

Jack, the brilliant omnipotent writer, began to edit
a lot of stuff out. He would be the hero getting the
senator three crisp pages just in time.

I would again be the failure would couldn't
manage the process.

Suddenly the Senator, visibly annoyed, entered
Jack's office.

"Where is it?" He was increasingly getting angry
feeding off of Jack's anger.

"Here." Jack had just hit print. "Here," he handed
it to him, "it's three pages."

I didn't want them to think I wasn't trying to
help. I peeked my head into Jack's office. "I requested
some additional floor time sir, just in case. You have
eight minutes now."

He didn't thank me. They never did. He just gave
me a dirty look and darted off to the Senate floor.

Jack stopped yelling at me. But that entire

afternoon I felt sick to my stomach. This was Jill's fault (and she like my other entitled legislative assistants had just asked us for raise), but I was technically her boss so I would take the fall for this one.

I got up quietly and went to the bathroom and covered my face as the tears started cascading down. I had only been there two years—not really enough time to quit—but I really didn't think I could take much more. When I got home late at night, I would just turn on classical music, drink wine and smoke cigarettes. I quit smoking after law school, but recently, due to all this stress, I had taken it up again.

I just knew this wasn't a healthy lifestyle or the life I wanted. But I just didn't know how to get out.

I heard my phone buzz.

"Everything okay today? I just saw your boss on the floor." Will texted.

Will was my colleague and my friend. He was also a Legislative Director to a Senator from the small state of Vermont, and besides cheese making, as far as I could tell there was very little going on in that state. His boss never went to the floor to speak on anything. I was really jealous. He has such an easy gig compared to me.

"It's a mess. In the bathroom. Can't stop crying." I texted back.

Will was my confidante. He knew how it went in my office, and he would never tell anyone. Everyone on the inside knew how Jack was, but it was like a dirty family secret that couldn't get out.

"Come up." He texted back.

His office was only one floor up from ours, and I spent a lot of time having meltdowns in there. Will was always calm and steady and willing to lend an ear. I admired that about him, but then what in the fuck did he have to be stressed about? He had a great looking successful boyfriend, an easy job, and a nice row house off of Dupont Circle. Charmed life, that one.

"Hi." I slid down on the chair in front of his desk. I felt the tears but held them back.

"So *what* is going on, Esme?" He leaned forward concerned.

"It's just getting worse and worse, Will." I paused.

"Jill that asshole didn't have her floor statement ready today. Jack was so pissed. It had to be three pages, and it was four. He threw the papers at me and then edited the whole thing himself."

"What the fuck? He threw the pages at you?"

"Yes… at my head… and last night we had drinks, and he asked me to come over to his apartment for a night cap. It's so fucked up." I buried my head in my hands.

"Are you kidding me?"

"No. No. I'm not."

"What are you going to do?"

"I don't know. I have no idea what to do. You know he can do anything."

"You have to report this, Esme. This is just crazy behavior. Our Chief would *never* do that. Never."

"I can't report it. I'll definitely get fired then. I don't even think the Senator likes me anymore. They are just waiting for something."

His phone buzzes.

"Listen, that's the Senator. I've got to take his. Hang in there. We'll talk later."

"Okay, thanks Will." I wiped under my eyes hoping my mascara hadn't smeared all over my cheeks. I was also hoping Jack wasn't looking for me. I should have been glued to the TV on my desk counting votes.

I slipped into my office where Jill thankfully was standing watching TV and counting the votes. I saw the "yah" votes were at 46 now. I felt relieved. We had only expected 41 so this was way better than I had expected. We all knew we wouldn't have the votes to pass it, but this was at least symbolic, and it showed we had garnered support.

Jack then stormed into my office. "Forty six! We only have 46! What the fuck?"

"The whip count two days ago had us at 41. We got five more." I responded calmly. I thought he would be pleased about our progress. But he never was. The only time he seemed kind of happy was when we were out drinking after work.

"This is pathetic!" He threw he arms up in the air and stared at me and Jill. "You should have done better. We're not going to get a second chance on this."

I didn't even care about climate change anymore. So what if we have melting glaciers in Antarctica? So what if we have more hurricanes lately? Who cares? I don't think they even cared about it really. It was just an artifice—to pass it and get him reelected this year.

"You," he pointed at me. "You and I are going to talk about this after work." And he stormed out. Why not talk it over with fucking Jill? It was her job to whip the votes and write the statement. I dreaded this conversation. And I knew it was going to be over drinks.

Six o'clock arrived. It was our official quitting time, and the staff started scurrying out the office for fear of getting summoned to the floor.

It was always this way. And then I would stay two or three hours later sometimes with very little to do.

"Come on," Jack came into my office slipping on his worn tweed blazer. "Let's go."

I shut off my computer and got up. I didn't know where we were going, but then, it really didn't matter. He was just going to drink and yell at me. Per usual.

When we got outside, he hailed a cab to the nearby restaurant, the George, which was a big Hill hang out. I thought it was kind of a dive, but Jack knew the owner, and they often would go outside and smoke together. He liked their Vodka tonics and the complimentary potato chips, and so I wasn't surprised when we ended up there.

This time he ordered a Vodka on the rocks. I knew this was serious. He then ordered me a Cab without even asking what I wanted.

At this point, I could have used a stiff drink, but the red wine would have to suffice.

"Listen," he began. "Today was a real mess. A real mess."

I listened and said nothing. There was no point to argue.

"And the Senator wasn't happy. I want you to know that."

My heart sank. I was hoping he didn't notice. I started to fear again that I would be fired. There were just too many things that had gone wrong. How was I going to pay my rent? My car? How was I going to get a new job? If I got fired, it surely would become public fast, and no one would hire me. He had me by the balls, and he knew it. I had to find some way to fix this at least temporarily.

"Well, I am sorry. I did the best I could."

"You should have managed Jill. She should have been writing all weekend."

"I told her to." I started to defend myself. "It's not my fault she went away all weekend! I can't chain her to her house."

"Regardless, there's just been too many fuck ups lately. I think the Senator may want something else. Someone different."

Jack was an elitist and so was the Ivy League-educated Senator. I just knew that they wanted someone from Harvard or Princeton and probably another woman. I knew one thing about Jack—he always hired women. He knew there was no way a man would put up with this shit. And he treated the men differently in our office. David, our foreign policy assistant, always received praise and accolades on his speeches. I never saw him scream at him. Craig who handled all the military issues often went rogue and advanced his own agenda not the Senator's, and he was never reprimanded.

"What do you mean someone different?" I felt the tears well up again. This wasn't the conversation I expected.

"Just someone different."

"Jack, I've been working my ass off for you. And the Senator... I don't know what more you want from me."

"Yes, I know. I just have to think about things."

I took a large sip of my wine. I looked at his clear glass over the table and realized I was drinking faster than him.

Then he abruptly changed the subject.

"Why don't we get out of here? Go to Calvin's for a bite?"

He was blowing my mind. Basically telling me I might be fired and then wanting to go eat? My stomach hurt so badly. I couldn't imagine eating a thing.

"I'm not hungry."

"Well, I am. Let's go." He motioned for the waiter to bring us our bill, but the owner shook his head. Once again, Jack would get off with free drinks.

Jack hailed a cab to Calvin's—a downtown oyster bar about seven blocks away. He often hung out there late at night because it was only one block from his apartment, and he could walk home.

"Table for two." He motioned to the hostess. Like everyone else in town, she knew him. And even though the restaurant was very busy and very loud, she found him a quiet round booth in the back.

He didn't talk anymore about my failure at work and possibly getting cashiered. This time he changed the subject to his wife. He began to tell me how dumb she was and how she didn't read the paper or have any interest in DC. He told me how all she wanted to do is play tennis all day and be with the girls.

"Well. We basically have an arrangement. She can do what she wants to do, and I can do what I want to do." He stated matter-of-factly.

I wasn't even sure how to respond to this. But it was starting to feel creepy.

"I mean I fly home to Idaho on the weekends, but I would rather just stay here. If it wasn't for the girls, I would."

I open the menu and look at entrees not because I'm hungry but because it is giving me something to do.

Jack then ordered another Vodka on the rocks.

"I'm fine." I motioned the waiter away.

"She'll have a Cab." He stated once again taking over my life.

I acquiesced. I admit although I knew this was very inappropriate and likely paid out of campaign funds, there was a part of me that really wanted another drink.

Jack went on to order a lot of food—crab cakes, calamari, and oysters on the half shell. Although I loved seafood, tonight I just had knots in my stomach. I kept thinking about what he said about wanting someone "different." I kept thinking, "What is wrong with me? I try so hard. Why don't they like me?"

As the Vodka poured down his throat, he became more brazen.

"How's that boyfriend of yours? Dump him yet?"

"I actually don't know. I haven't seen him much lately." I want to say "Due to you asshole, I never see my boyfriend who I just know is teetering on breaking up with me."

"You can do better Esme. I wouldn't waste my time with that asshole."

Jack didn't even know Evan. My Senator wasn't that involved in technology issues. He didn't sit on the relevant committee, and he came from a state that was more interested in agriculture and environmental issues so I had no idea where this was coming from.

"You don't even know him, Jack." I felt myself defending Evan.

"Well... I know of him, and that's enough."

I rolled my eyes. There was no arguing with him.

"Eat!" He said handing me an oyster. I obediently

157

ate it. I just wanted to eat the food and get the hell out of there. As we finished eating most of the meal, the waiter came over and cleared the table. I felt relief because now I could finally go home.

Then he said it. I couldn't believe it. I still can't, but it really happened.

"Why don't we go back to my apartment and open up that Cab?"

"Jack, I really have to get home. I have a long day tomorrow."

"Just one drink. I promise. You will love this wine."

"I'm done drinking. I've had enough."

He looked at me intensely like a child wanting a bright shiny object. He smiled.

"I'm really horny. Let's go back to my place."

"That's very inappropriate, Jack." I couldn't believe this. I had had enough.

"Oh come on, I'm just kidding around. But you should come over. I'll show you the kitchen I just remodeled."

"I have to go now." I stood up and grabbed my purse. I almost ran out of the restaurant. I felt like he was after me, and this wasn't going to stop no matter what I did.

* * *

Two days passed. I couldn't stop thinking about that evening and that comment—and the other comments, in fact. It triggered a lot of anxiety in me because it brought back memories of what had happened to me ten years ago in the law firm. I thought often about that experience and how I did nothing about it because I was afraid. I didn't want to be afraid anymore. Plus it looked like I was going to lose my job anyway. I talked to Will a lot during those days. He encouraged me strongly to go to the Senate legal counsel. I was 37 now, not 27. I realized I had to go.

I knew I had to be careful though. I had to sneak to the Office of Compliance, which just happened to be on the basement level of our building. There was no way anyone could see me walk in there. I also was *never* away from my desk that long so I had to tell Jack I was going to get an allergy shot.

As I waited anxiously in the lobby area, a tall slim woman with black hair tied neatly in a bun came over to me and introduced herself. She told me to come into to her office.

When I told her about the comment and the other comments and all of it really, she looked at me calmly and stopped jotting down notes on her yellow pad.

"When exactly did this happen?"

"Two nights ago."

"Okay. That's good. You came quickly. You only have six months to bring a claim here."

I had no idea. I was relieved I had acted quickly. We went on to discuss the situation in detail. She never seemed shocked or supportive.

It was almost like she didn't care.

"Well, here is the process we have here. You have reported a claim of sexual harassment. We now require you to go to counseling for a month. Then there will be a cooling off period... for you to reflect on things... to decide if you want to go forward. If you do decide to pursue the claim, you will be required to go to mediation, and a mediator will decide on the merits of the case."

"*I* have to go to counseling?"

"Yes. That's a requirement pursuant to Senate rules."

"Unbelievable. Why doesn't he have to go to counseling? He's the nutjob."

"It's only 30 days, and everything discussed is strictly confidential."

"I don't want to go to counseling. I don't need counseling."

"That's the process, Esme. It's mandatory. And I just want to caution you—you *will* be suing the office of the Senator. Legally, you are not directly suing the senator himself… but essentially you are."

I leave the office in a rage. Suing the senator? How could I possibly do that? What would become of me? And how am I going to go through mediation? I can't afford a lawyer.

I walk up the three floors of marble stairs and stop in Will's office. I tell him about the conversation and ask for his advice.

"Sue him. You'll get a settlement out it anyway. It won't go public." He says as he leans back in his oversized leather chair.

"I don't want a settlement!"

"Yes. Yes you do."

"No, I just want it to stop. I want him to leave me alone… and I want to protect other women from this happening again. I walked away from this last time it happened. I don't want to do that again."

"I know this happened to you before, Esme. But

this is the United States Senate for Chris sakes. You have to be careful. There's a lot at stake."

Will appears to be changing his mind, and he is scaring me.

"I know." I rub my fingers through my hair and then bury my head in my hands. "And it's basically his word against mine."

I go home that night and pour a glass of wine and call Evan. We talk about the situation at length, and he of course thinks I should go forward with the claim. He's a guy though and a real ball buster at that. I don't think he has an appreciation of how difficult this will be for me, and it might be an insurmountable challenge. Jack is powerful. And he's persuasive. I wonder if anyone, including the mediator, would even believe me.

In the end, after much reflection, I decide I cannot go forward with the claim. I feel weak. I'm disappointed in myself. But more than that, I'm afraid. Afraid of Jack. Afraid of the Senator. Afraid it will get out and ruin my reputation forever. I don't want a settlement. I just want it to stop. But it doesn't and it probably never well.

In the end, I do just what Evan said I should do. I quit the Senate, which I loved and go into the private sector to be a lobbyist and make some money. I capitulate and take a job I know I will likely hate. Jack will end up staying there for 11 more years until he retires with a full pension.

About the Author

Esme Oliver is the author of *Smoke, Drink F*#K* -- an acclaimed romance novel about an intense affair between a woman on the precipice of turning 40 and a much younger chef she meets on a trip to Todi, Italy. While the romance starts out as a meaningless fling, it later advances into a relationship with plans for the two to reunite again in Portugal. However, unbeknownst to Esme, her love has made other plans to fly to Istanbul without her leaving her ghosted across the world. *Smoke Drink F*#K* has been featured in Bustle, the Huffington Post and NPR.

Esme Oliver has worked as an attorney, a health-care lobbyist, and a legislative director for two US Senators; work which sharpened her left brain but didn't quite fulfill her soul. Esme eventually left DC for her native Midwest, where she now writes grants (for money) and stories (for fun). She enjoys lots of travel and a long list of other activities that pair well with a nice Pinot.

Other Riverdale Avenue Books You Might Enjoy

Smoke, Drink, F*#K
By Esme Oliver

#MeToo:
Essays About How and Why This Happened, What It
Means and How to Make Sure
It Never Happens Again.
Edited By Lori Perkins

The Princess of 42nd Street:
Surviving My Childhood as The Daughter of Paul
Square's King of Porn
By Romola Hodas

Flashes: Adventures in Dating Through Menopause
By Michelle Churchill

Confessions of a Librarian: Memoirs of Loves
By Barbra Foster

The Secret Life of EL James: The Unauthorized
Biography
By Marc Shapiro

Naked in 30 Days: A One-Month Guide to Getting Your Mind, Body and Soul
By Theresa Roemer

Shattered: The Rise & Fall & Rise of a Wrestling Diva
By Tamara "Sunny" Sytch

Lightning Source UK Ltd.
Milton Keynes UK
UKHW022023150519
342718UK00008B/777/P